Soho

Rob Adam

Acknowledgements

To my extended family who have given their love, support, and most importantly their patience throughout this, my first publication. I thank you from the bottom of my heart. I apologise in advance for anyone that I may forget to mention.. But remember...there is always book number two.

So, here goes: To Glen and Liz, for being the first to support my transition to literature.

To Dawn and Julian for making me think about the continuity and the importance of attention to detail.

To Janet, Sandra, Sue (times four) Gill and Maxine for pushing me to write every chapter consistently and to never lose momentum whilst also being open to learning new experiences. (nudge , nudge girls).

To Zoe and Sam , for their unending enthusiasm, nurture, and consistent belief in me that I had a story to tell, I thank you so deeply.

To Abi, for being the first to finish the book, for loving the characters, and for loving the all important twist.

To everyone else (Becky, Tess, Lisa, the list goes on) who took the leap of faith to buy the book on the basis of a first chapter.. Always know how blessed, and humbled I feel to have your support.

And finally to Diaz: thank you for making me the happiest man alive, you're my strength, my source of inspiration, my Mr Right...my Kez.

CHAPTER 1

" Maria, you bitch! That's hardly fair! " Says Theo, choking on his glass of red wine. " I mean - Yes, granted, Andrew can be a little self involved at times, but then again who isn't? "

Maria lifts her glass to her lips, her beautiful dark brown eyes, wide in disbelief.

" Oh please T! A little self involved? That's like saying Wasabi is a little bit hot, or that porn is a little bit sexual. " She pauses to take another sip before looking directly at him. " Or that you're a little bit gay!! "

Theo stares back, mouth open. His own expression mocking her incredulous look.

" Or that you're a little bit loose! " He says pointing at her crotch.

Maria jolts upright causing her to throw the contents of the glass of cabernet sauvignon she is holding, across her freshly painted ruby red feature wall. The two look at each other, then at the empty glass and the wine splattered wall, then collapse into fits of laughter.

After a few minutes Maria recomposes herself, grabs a wet cloth and mops the wall gently, her expression now changes from feigned indignation at Theo's previous comment, to concern.

" Seriously though Theo, do you really see this thing with Andrew going somewhere? I look at you; this sincere, caring, intelligent articulate man and then I look at him." She pauses. " I can't help but think are you on crack or just horny, or for that matter, both? "

Theo smiles weakly, takes one of the chicken strips from the selection of appetisers Maria has meticulously arranged on her black Italian designer glass table, and crams it into his mouth. He gestures toward his now full mouth and chews contemplatively for a few minutes before uttering. " Maria, he's really there for me."

Maria raises one eyebrow. " There for you when you have money, more like. " Her eyes narrow inquisitively, her voice softens. " Oh ,and don't think for one minute that I didn't realise what you just did? "

Theo shrugs his shoulders unconvincingly.

" I have known you for years, babe, don't try and pull that angelic shit on me.... You filled your face with food to buy yourself some extra time. "

He looks back at her, still puzzled.

" Extra time to think of one thing, just one redeeming thing to say about Andrew. Believe me, you'll have more chance of finding one iota of merit in Maria Carey's performance in Glitter than any measure of sincerity in one molecule of him. " She pauses for a moment, "All I'm saying is, if you have to think about it... " She takes another sip, this time to let the gravity of her statement settle.

Theo stares into his empty wine glass, his hands steady, his eyes fixated. A few moments pass in silence, then his hand starts to shake and his once, still body, trembles. Tears form in his eyes before dispersing, leaving warm wet tracks down his face.

Maria stumbles across the floor of her newly furnished, albeit slightly wine stained, London Soho apartment to join him on the sofa.

" Sweetness I'm sorry, the last thing in the world I want to do is upset you. " Her hand gently strokes the back of his head, " It's just that I see the way you fall so quickly, and so hard for that matter, and, I have to be honest with you T, nine times out of ten you have absolutely nothing in common with the guy except that you are both men. "

Maria continues to stroke his hair, starting from the top of his head to the nape of his neck. This always eased his pain. Maria had learned very early on in the ten years worth of his countless disastrous relationships that he had always responded well to tactile behaviour. This simple action was all it took to soothe him.

Theo dries his eyes with his shirt sleeve, takes a deep breath, and forces a smile. " We both love cock too. "

She laughs, relieved that she hasn't ruined his night with her brutal honesty. " Oh now I see, it's all about the cock. His cock is what keeps you coming back for more! "

" Um, kettle.. pot...black...Stuart, Marcus, Darius, Kelvin, Thom.. " He says counting on each finger.

She silences him mid sentence with her hand. " Okay, okay, point taken..Oh and by the way, I prefer the term flexible. "

" Flexible? " He says.

" I'm flexible.. not loose. " She grins.

Maria's attitude to sex had always been, for want of a better word, liberated. Whilst most of the kids at her school were taking their first tentative steps into teen romances, boys and french kissing, she was mastering the art of giving perfect hand jobs and was well versed in everything oral. This made her unsurprisingly infamous with the school's prepubescent male population. In fact, she was popular with all things testosterone related. Even the teachers had a soft spot for her unmistakeable Latin good looks. All she had to do in class was lean forward, play seductively with her long black hair, and push her well developed breasts towards the sky, and in their eyes, she could do no wrong.

Yes, it was safe to say that Maria was never short of male attention.

The girls, on the other hand, were a totally different story. They had mistakenly associated her sexual confidence with arrogance, choosing to believe that she considered herself above them and too mature to have time for them. This couldn't have been further from the truth. Growing up, the one thing that Maria had craved was connection, something real, something tangible. A true soulmate. It wasn't until she turned eighteen, on her first day at Exeter University, that she finally found this in Theo.

Theo stood out from the crowd. He had an optimistic air about him. Much in the same way that Maria had been misunderstood throughout her school years, Theo, for different reasons had suffered a similar fate. The other students thought he was incredibly naive. They couldn't understand how he had remained so un- jaded, so unashamedly ' up ' all the time. Inevitably this rare out look on life attracted some very unwanted attention in the form of one boy.

Kieran Jameson.

Kieran was determined to bring Theo down at every opportunity. The extent of this harassment could only be described as bullying. Even though it hurt Theo, he would always remember the encouraging words his parents would say to him when he returned from his school, located in Langport, Somerset. They would say that he should try to be the best of friends with this boy because he was just misunderstood and all he needed was love. Therein lay the reason for Theo's ever positive state of mind. His parents.

They were the kind of people who could always put a good spin on any given situation. If an exam had been failed, then it was a trial run for better things in the future.

Then when his grandparents announced their divorce on his thirteenth birthday, they pitched it as a life affirming lesson in love and its potential pitfalls.

Even when his beloved mother passed away , his dad had said it was an insight into the importance of appreciating every second that we are alive on this earth.

His attitude to life meant that when he hit his mid twenties and started working at Bar Soho, a funky, diverse gay bar, the carefree attitude that had once disadvantaged him, soon became his biggest asset. The punters loved him.

To the women, he gave a new perspective. A hope, that if they looked hard enough they would find a nice guy, a nice guy just like Theo. Of course they knew he was gay, but this didn't matter. It was enough for them to believe there were good men out there just like him and not the usual walking wastes of space.

To the guys, or at least the gay guys, he was a breath of fresh air. He was the opposite of everything typically scene. No cynicism, no ulterior sexual motives, just beautiful inside and out. Drawn to his carefree attitude and good humour, Theo was never without a date on a Saturday night, or any night of the week for that matter.

Inevitably, there was a downside to his cheerful disposition in his adult life, because although he could attract anyone, his unwavering belief in seeing the good in everybody led to him being taken advantage of countless times. The latest man to do this being Andrew.

Theo first met Andrew on the London underground. Well, technically their eyes met and they shared a five minute love affair on the journey from Covent Garden to Piccadilly Circus. Andrew had joined the train in a blur, his right foot only just clearing the doors before they shut behind him. He took the only seat left on the busy carriage opposite him. Theo hadn't noticed him at first as he had had his eyes closed, immersed in the contents of his iPod as he had always done on his way to work. It was only when he felt a foot graze his shoe that he opened his eyes. The man in front of him was a tall man. This wasn't immediately apparent and had only realised it when his foot had touched his. His tanned skin was darker than Theo's olive complexion and his athletic frame, wide shoulders and tightly fitting blue-grey T-Shirt showed off a well defined midriff. His chestnut eyes sparkled with humour, but in contrast, his slightly parted mouth showed no emotion. Nevertheless Andrew was a very striking man. Theo looked deep into his intense penetrating eyes for what seemed like an eternity. In reality it was nothing more than ten seconds, but it was enough time to stir more than just his emotions. He soon realised that the smile that was creeping across the strangers face was not out of friendliness but was in recognition of the erection that had appeared beneath Theo's trousers. He quickly covered his shame with his jacket and hoped that it would be fading before the next stop. Unfortunately, the more he concentrated, the harder it became. The next stop arrived and the man departed, his smile never fading as he watched the train leave for it's next destination. Theo feeling so relieved that the man had gone, hadn't seen that that stop was in fact *his* stop.

He quickly disembarked at the next station, exited the underground, and raced across the street, to arrive at Note Perfect albeit ten minutes late. He made his apologies, quickly changed into the bars black T-Shirt with, and served his first drink of the night.. to the stranger on the tube.

After a full minute of wishing that the ground would swallow him up, Theo brushed aside his humiliation and mixed the stranger's Strawberry Daiquiri serving it with acute precision. Believing that he had succeeded in regaining some semblance of dignity through his professionalism, he looked him squarely in the eyes and asked if there would be anything else. He politely declined with his hand and shook his head simultaneously. Theo, feeling confident that the previous embarrassing experience on the underground was as far in the distance as the train itself, turned his back on the stranger and shifted attention to the nearest customer.

Whilst serving the next two customers drinks, he couldn't help but notice the stranger's hand extended firmly in the air, vying for his attention. Knowing that it was more than his job's worth to continue to ignore him, he smiled openly and approached him.

" Yes, what can I get you sir? " He asked.

" I would like a long soft comfortable screw up against the wall please." He said, with a straight face.

Theo tried to remain unflinching, but within seconds he was blushing furiously. Just as he thought he was about to burst into flames, a wry smile crept across the strangers face and he extended his hand out to Theo.

" Please forgive me, I couldn't resist it. I'm Andrew, it's nice to meet you..? "

Theo obliged and filled in the gap. " Theo, I'm Theo, or as my friends know me, T."

Within moments, Theo's awkwardness was replaced by the original attraction he had felt on the underground. Sure enough, six hours and eight drinks later, it was Andrew that was serving Theo a ' screwdriver ' of a very different kind in the back room of the bar after closing time.

" So, enough about me and my terminally ill love life, how are things going with you and Chris? You haven't mentioned him all night? " He says, opening another bottle of cabernet sauvignon and refilling his glass.

" Chris is Chris, nothing more, nothing less. He is a really nice guy, we just haven't managed to find a base connection yet, but it's early days, so we'll see ." She gestures with her glass for some more wine.

Theo chastises her playfully with his index finger. " I don't think so Maria, no talk, no wine! "

" What do you mean? " She says, pushing her glass under the bottle. " You asked me, I told you. There just really isn't much to tell. We have gone on a few dates, nice food, polite conversation, just standard date stuff. Now, are you going to give me some more wine, or am I going to have to rugby tackle you for it! "

He pulls the bottle away from her glass, covering it with his hand.

" Once again, *I repeat*, I don't think so. You've grilled me like a George Foreman all night long over Andrew and all you can give me is surface stuff. " He says defiantly.

" That's because that is all there has been, just ' surface stuff. ' Now, can we *please* move on."

" No, no, no, there's something you're not telling me." He lifts the glass to his lips taunting her as he takes a sip. " Or did you forget that I know *you* just as well too! When you start dating a guy for the first time you normally can't stop talking about him, which leads me to believe somethings up. So, details please! "

" Details?? You want details?? Okay here goes! "

Maria takes a deep breath.

" He likes music from the eighties and anything electro infused from the nineties, he plays football every Wednesday followed by a few pints at The Red Dragon Inn, but no longer than an hour so that he can get home in time to watch CSI. He likes Indian food, but only orders from the sub standard takeaway up the road so as to avoid delivery charges. He works as a security man as does his best friend since childhood, Martin, who also plays football on Wednesday. He hates driving in the rain, eating after seven o clock, hospital dramas and airports.. " She taps her chin in exaggeration. " Oh, and there's something I'm forgetting. I can't think for the life of me what it is.... Oh, oh, oh, I remember... *He's the worst sex I have ever had! Now* can I have some wine?? "

Maria's first meeting with Chris was evidently nowhere near as sexually fulfilling as Theo and Andrew's, but, nonetheless, it was equally eventful.
  She had been staying late at the office for the fifth consecutive night to meet deadlines in a vain attempt to achieve recognition from her inattentive manager. She was just finishing her sixth cup of coffee of the day and was about to go for her tenth loo break when her mobile rang. It was her sister Amelia, which was unexpected considering they had never been close.
The last time she had contacted Maria was to tell her that she was pregnant.. Nine months pregnant to be

exact, and that her water had just broke and needed a lift to the hospital and pretty damn quick.

" Um, hey Amy, how can I help? " She said tentatively.

" Relax Maria, unclench, I can hear it in your voice! I'm not going to tell you I'm pregnant again." She joked.

Maria released the grip from her phone slightly. " That is a relief to hear, but to be honest, I was expecting much worse this time." She said as she made her way to the toilets.

" Oh come on sis, what could possibly be worse than me telling you that I'm sitting in a pool of my own amniotic fluid and about to push a person out of my vagina? "

" Oh I don't know, maybe that your six month old, Leigh has moved to Hollywood to pursue a modelling career. "

" Very funny Maria! " She said sarcastically, " Now, if you wouldn't mind I have something I need to ask you."

There was a long pause. Long enough for Maria to check the reception of the phone in case the call had dropped.

" I'm getting married. Would you be my bridesmaid?? " Amelia asked.

Maria froze. She took a deep breath and held it whilst opening the door to the last cubicle in the toilet. She closed the door firmly and turned the lock.

" Umm, well, sure, I..I..I mean, that would be..nice. "

" Phew! Good good! Well, it's decided, you should come over to the house tomorrow. We'll have a day of it, dress shopping in the afternoon, cocktails and sushi in the evening you can meet my maid of honour, it will be wonderful, just us girls etc. "

Maria sat in shock, a million thoughts racing through her head. *Amelia?? Married???? More to the point, with who?? I didn't even know she was seeing anyone!? Has she got back with Leigh's father? Surely it couldn't have been going on for long otherwise I would have heard all about it from mum at our monthly coffee at Costa. Unless, she hasn't even told mum! No, that can't be it. She couldn't keep anything secret even if she wanted to, her mouth is too big, and, besides, she loves the attention she gets from shocking people with her latest revelations.*

" Hello? Are you there? "

Maria had totally forgotten she was still on the phone.

" Maria, If you're still there, I have to go. I think I can hear Leigh grizzling, she's teething at the moment, and they are growing at such an alarming rate. If I'm not careful she'll start chewing her own fingers off. Just be at my place at ten then we can get an early start. Bye for now sis! "   The phone disconnected abruptly before Maria had a chance to say goodbye.

She listened to the dead tone for a minute, still stunned, and still trying to process the conversation that had just taken place. She slowly stood up. *Why was she telling me? Why does she thrive on the drama? Why can't she just slow down for once in her life?* She tried the handle, nothing. *And why can't I open this door?* She tried again, this time with force. *Oh God! why can't I open the door????* 'She gripped the door, this time with more force, and shook.

" Help! is there anyone there!! "

She knew there wasn't anyone around in the office at this time of night, but rational thought was the last thing on her mind. All she could think about was the probability that she would be using the toilet roll as a pillow and the toilet seat as a head board tonight if she didn't get out.

" Is anybody there?! " She whimpered half heartedly." Anyone?? "

She slumped onto the toilet, her phone still in hand. *My phone!* She thought suddenly. She dialled Theo's number carefully and waited for the ringing tone. " Come on T! Pick up, pick up! "

" Hello? " A voice answered. " Are you okay? "

" T? " She said, confused.

It was then that she realised that the voice wasn't coming from the other end of the phone, but outside the toilet cubicle.

" Hello Ms, it's Chris, the security guard. "

Chris, Perfect! She thought, fumbling around her Prada handbag for her make-up mirror. *Of all the people that could have found me unprepared like this, it had to be him!*

Maria's attraction to Chris had started on her first day working at Johnson & Richardson when she had bumped into him, quite literally, whilst exiting the lift to her floor. His muscular chest was the first thing she had felt as her face ploughed into it, closely followed by his equally toned abdominals whilst reaching out her hands to steady herself.

Maria, being Maria had not been embarrassed by the close contact though. In fact, she relished every second, letting her fingers linger seductively on his shirt, her eyes slowly moving upwards until they connected with his. The first thing she noticed was how kind his face was. He had a warmth that she didn't associate with someone in his profession. His eyes were big and round with well worn laughter lines. His lips were full and soft and even though he was not smiling at the time, she knew he would have a killer one when he did.

She pulled away from him swiftly, made her apologies and continued on her way. All the while, ensuring that she didn't show any sign of weakness, never once looking back at him. She wanted to maintain the mystery, like the latest fragrance to come out of Paris. Her plan, up until now, had not been successful, but things were about to change.

" Hi Chris, it's me, Maria. Don't ask me how, but I have somehow managed to lock myself in! " She said, in the calmest voice she could muster.

" Believe me Ms Martinez, you're not the first person to get stuck in this cubicle. Facilities were supposed to get it fixed ages ago. "

Ms Martinez? How does he know my surname? I'm sure I've never told him? She rummaged around in her hand bag, this time for her mascara. *He must have asked someone, and if he has asked, that means he must be interested in me after all!* She adjusted her cleavage and undid an extra button on her blouse. *Looks like coordinating my wardrobe to wear my three best bras on the same days he works, has finally paid off.*

She stood up. " Thank you Chris, I thought I was going to be here all night. Oh, and please, call me Maria, none of this Ms Martinez anymore okay? "

" Okay Maria, I'll soon have you out of there. " He boomed.

She sat back down on the toilet and waited.

A few moments passed and then she heard Chris's deep voice again.

" Okay, that should do it, I'm coming in! " Chris said as the door flung open to reveal an embarrassed Maria.

He took one look at her and said. " You do realise, if you wanted to get me alone, you only had to ask! "

Within seconds, the tension in the air fluttered away, and Maria and Chris looked at each other knowingly and laughed.

" Worst sex you have ever had ! Oh My! " Theo says, his hand covering his mouth in genuine surprise, " I am so sorry that I withheld wine from you at such a serious time. " He hastily fills her glass right to the top before doing the same with his. " So, how, where? " He stops for a moment, " and when did you find out? "

Theo listens intently to Maria as she regales the story of how she and Chris met, and the lead up to the night she was trapped in the toilet at work.

" That must have been so awkward! " He says, munching on a deep fried Camembert before changing the subject. " Now, don't get me wrong hun, because I'm glad that you are finally sharing with me things about Chris, but, this still doesn't explain when you found out he was bad in bed?..or was it that night? "

She nods.

" After you finished work, few drinks, back to his place? One thing led to another? " He says encouragingly.

She shakes her head from side to side.

" Did you? " He waits dramatically. " No, you didn't ! You *did*, didn't you??! "

Maria looks away from him, trying not to smile. She turns her head back, her eyes meet his, and she nods confidently.

Theo stands up and starts to clap. " And the award for the sluttiest sex act goes to Maria Martinez for her scene in Toilet Fuck! "

Maria throws a pillow at his stomach. " Ha, ha, very funny T! Well, it would have been if what happened next wasn't so..tragic. "

" Aww babe, " He says reassuringly, " It can't have been that bad. The first time with someone new *can* be disappointing. You have all these expectations about how it's going to be and they rarely end up being like the image you have in your head. " He says as he sits down next to her. " What was it? Is he too rough? Not rough enough? " He says winking.

" No it's his dick. It's no more than three inches inches long! " She says flatly.

" You mean flaccid, right? " His voice urgent. " Please, tell me you mean flaccid? "

She falls into his lap, exasperated. " No, un-erect he is two inches long. "

" Wow! I guess I'm going to have to start calling you Bridget Boneless from now on! " He says, without thinking.

" Theo! I'm being serious here. " She picks herself up from his lap and unwittingly picks up a phallic shaped cheese straw before dropping it back on the table. " At first, I thought maybe he's lost his erection and that's why I cant feel him, but then I looked at the expression on his face and he had that look. You know, that look that porn stars have on their face just before the obligatory cum shot, and then I knew I was wrong. " She looks at Theo, unimpressed. " Oh, and he kept saying, ' Take it baby, take it all! ' " She says mimicking his voice. " I had to bite my lip to stop myself from saying, " Love, the only thing I can take right now, is the piss out of your tiny excuse for a dick! "

Theo snorts as his glass reaches his lips. He reaches over and takes her hand. " So, reality check, I have to ask. Why are you still seeing the guy? Did you not think to end it then and there? If it was anybody else I would be advising that there is more to a relationship than just sex, but it's you we're talking about. I mean politically correct bullshit aside, you are a sexually driven woman, Maria. You without sex is like Robbie Williams rapping, it just doesn't work. The thing is that- "

A knock at the door stops Theo mid sentence.

" That's weird, I'm not expecting anyone? Are you? " Maria steadies herself up using the arm of the couch and walks towards the hallway.

" Maybe it's the dick police wanting to talk to your boyfriend about his criminally small pee pee. " Shouts Theo drunkenly.

Maria's laughter soon trails off at the sight of her sister, standing in the doorway, makeup running down her face.

" Amelia? Are you okay? " She has never seen her sister like this.

" I didn't know where else to go Maria. " She sobs.

" You're scaring me Amelia, what's happened? Where's Leigh? "

" She's okay, she's at home with Tom.. my fiancé. " She wipes her nose on her coat sleeve. " Oh Maria, I have gotten myself into such a mess. "

Maria wraps her arms around her and leads her into the apartment. " Whatever it is, we can sort it out, ok? "

CHAPTER 2

The sudden change in temperature from the warm confines of Maria's cosy apartment to the cool autumnal breeze outside, almost instantly sobers Theo. He had decided to tactfully excuse himself and leave after seeing the state of Amelia's mascara smudged face at the door.

Whatever it is, it must be pretty big for her to turn up like that, unannounced..and crying, too! This is a woman who is normally made of stone! She didn't even shed a tear when we watched The Green Mile at the cinema. In fact, if I recall correctly, whilst everyone in the cinema was in floods of tears when John Coffey is about to be plunged into darkness before his execution and he says, " Don't put me in the dark, I is afraid of the dark. " She yawned!

He crosses the road and heads towards Bar Italia, an all night cafe in Berwick Street, to re-evaluate what to do with the rest of his night.

The smell of fresh coffee wafting in front of him as he nears, reminds him of how much he's had to drink and how little food he has eaten. Deciding that a prosciutto panini should satisfy his hunger, he approaches the door and walks into the starkly lit cafe and approaches the counter.

He looks along the elongated room, it's pale yellow and dark maroon stripes uniformly stretching to the back of the cafe, whilst it's mismatched flooring attempts to follow suit unsuccessfully with it's own pattern. Whilst he waits for the assistant to take his order, he can't help but feel the overall ambience of the place is more akin to a barbers shop than any late night spot. With it's old pictures and memorabilia on the wall behind the counter and the unending mirrors dominating the opposite, the only thing missing is the low drone of a pair of clippers.

As he scans the room for a spare stool or chair, he takes a moment to look at the people populating the room. In the corner, what appears to be a newly formed couple, beam at each other, smiling from ear to ear. They stare longingly into each others eyes as they fumble their words awkwardly. A group of older gents, stood under the functional television screen, drink espressos each one boasting a story more fantastical than the last. Some late night club goers talk loudly, oblivious that they no longer need to shout above the music that has filled their ears in the pubs and clubs of Soho. Theo takes a seat by the window and waits for his food all the while people watching, absorbing.

Of all the people in the room though, it is the aforementioned couple that holds his attention. He looks on wistfully, losing himself in nostalgic thought. He reminisces about his first ' date ' with Andrew and their first passionate, lingering kiss. He thinks about the first time their hands touched, and the intensity he felt with every contact after. He remembers the first time he felt Andrew's strong hands gripping his chest, the first time he felt him deep inside him.

As he sits, watching the attraction grow between the two strangers, it suddenly hits him. The cold undeniable truth. Why had he not seen it before? The connection between he and Andrew, was no deeper than that of the couple across the room. It was still at its most basic, its most sexual. It's most animal. He takes a breath.

Maria is right. I am concentrating too much on the physicality between Andrew and I. He looks back at the couple, entranced by their affinity. *No, that can't be right! Surely I would have seen it. Wouldn't I? It's not like I'm some generic teenager with immature, under developed emotional responses... Am I ?*

The tall, cheerful looking counter assistant approaches him and places his food in front of him. He thanks him graciously and continues to deconstruct his thoughts. *No, surely we do do things together that don't involve sex, don't we?* He takes a bite of the delicious piping hot sandwich. *Well, we do go out for dinner.* He chews slowly. *Although we don't really have much to say to each other when we get there. It's just the usual: His job, his family, his football team, his job again, and then back to how he is going to fuck me later on.*

We just go through the motions...

The sound of his phone ringing, more intense with every realisation of the inadequacies of his relationship, knocks him back to reality with a bump.

" Hello? " He says disconnectedly.

" You can do better than that T! " A highly animated voice booms down the phone, demanding attention. " Let's try that again. Repeat after me. ' Callum! Where have you been? Geez, I've missed your laugh, your smile, your movie star good looks, your cheeky banter! Your sexy black ass. ' Ready? "

" Callum where you been? He says, still preoccupied by his revelations. " Geez, I've missed your.. "

The voice on the phone stops him mid sentence. " Right! I don't know *who* the fuck you are, but what have you done with my friend, Theo!? You had better give him back bitch or I'm gonna come down there and *break* you.. "

" Ha, ha, very funny Callum, " He says, his trance breaking slightly. " I actually have missed you. Where have you been? "

" Me? Mainly bed hopping from man to man in east London, how about you? Still seeing Andrew? "

" Uh huh. " He says weakly taking another bite.

" That's it! You and I are going for a drink.. now! I don't know where you are, or what you're doing, and I don't give a rat's ass about either. Something's clearly eating you, and not in the good way, and I'm guessing it's because of mister not - so - wonderful himself. So, be at Floridita on Wardour Street in two minutes. No stalling. No excuses. No comebacks. Be there! " Then the phone was dead.

Theo, relieved for the temporary distraction, smiles to himself.

" Well, at least I know what I'm doing with the rest of my night." He says out loud to himself as he finishes his food.

I guess it makes sense, since Andrew's flat is on Hanover Square and won't take me more than ten minutes walk and I need to address the issue, and air my concerns.

He catches the waiters eye and nods his head goodbye, takes one last lingering glance back at the couple, and walks back out into the cold streets again.

A five minute walk later, Theo arrives at the bar and restaurant , energised from the food, and excited to see his friend Callum. As he walks along the street dominated by the sophisticated black and white awnings leading up to the steps to the glass doors, fond memories come flooding back to him. The two abstract figures dancing on the wall towering to the left, set against a light turquoise background now taking on new meaning. This had been the place where Callum and he had first met and danced together.

It had been an average Thursday night, and the guys from work had decided they needed to have some drinks to let off steam after a particularly difficult day at the bar. They had heard about a popular Latin American place with the added bonus of a live band.

Theo, being no stranger to charming his way onto stage and performing, had negotiated with the bar staff a one off performance with the house band. He had requested the somewhat obvious choice of Justin Timberlake's Señorita.

A few minutes later he was called to the front. One verse in, he was unexpectedly joined on stage by a short handsome black man who began to grind his body up against him. Theo, unfazed, responded by turning his back on him, letting his body yield to him. Every minute passing, their moves became more erotic, more sexually charged and by the time the song had finished, the dancing was practically pornographic.

Theo felt he had found his match. His ideal. It was only when the two of them had stumbled back to Callum's apartment that they both realised this couldn't have been further from the truth. The build up was promising. The kisses, passionate, eager with anticipation. It was only when Theo removed his jeans to reveal his black briefs with the words 'INSERT HERE' accompanied by an arrow pointing towards his ass that Callum took a step back. Theo, hurriedly pulled his jeans back on, alarmed that his novelty underwear had offended. It was then that Theo realised why Callum had lost his momentum.

Callum had sheepishly removed his khakis only to show a pair of boxers with pink writing stamped across his bottom that read THIS WAY IN.

An awkward silence, followed by unrestrained laughter, later and the two re dressed themselves.

" Oh well! Since neither of us are going to spend the night *fucking*, I guess there's nothing else left to do except for us to get *fucked* ! " Said Callum resignedly as he helped himself to a beer from the portable fridge Theo kept in the bedroom. As the two of them drank into the early hours of the morning, so began a beautiful new day to match their beautiful new friendship.

" Theodore! There you are! What time do you call this? I thought I told you two minutes bitch, not five ! Anyone would have thought you took a bus here ! " A voice from across the room at the bar, bellows.

Theo walks towards his friend, the   multitude of bottles of rum and exotic spirits, illuminated by the playful neon lit red and blue sign, excites his senses. " Actually I did take the bus here. " He says mockingly.

He hands Theo a Mary Pickford, a sublime mix of spiced rum, pineapple , lime and grenadine with a dash of cherry liqueur. " I'm just saying if it was me, I would have made it here on time, that's all. " He grins cheekily.

" Ah, well, that's the difference between you and I. *Clearly* I haven't taken a bus here, but if I *had*, I certainly wouldn't have been prepared to fuck the driver to get what I want! " He says wryly taking a swig of his much needed drink.

Callum gets up from his seat and hugs Theo fiercely, " That's the man I know and love! " He says kissing him on his neck. " And actually, if you must know, *I did.* "

" Did what? "

" Naughty things with a bus driver. Last Tuesday night on the way back from work. " He says proudly.

" Oh my! " Theo rolls his eyes.

" Don't judge! He'd finished for the night so I finished *him* for the night. " He says wiping the side of his mouth, grinning.

Theo smiles shaking his head at him.

" What?? It's not like I slept with him."

" Really? Why not, that's not like you at all." He says surprised.

" Well, to be fair I had every intention to, but then I saw his finger nails. Believe me, there was no way I was letting those things anywhere near my ass! Edward Scissorhands has nothing on him! " He shivers at the recollection of the memory.

" Anyway, enough about me and my fantastic existence, how are you babe? "

" I don't know, I guess.. I'm.. " He stumbles for the words.

" Average, sub standard, mediocre.. and if I may say so, desperately in need of a tan! " He says filling in the gaps.

He shifts from facing Callum, to leaning his back on the mahogany coloured bar." I'm good *actually*. Honestly, I have my health, a job, good friends, I'm thankful for what I have. "

Callum gestures towards the two shot glasses, and they both knock back a Tequila shot. " It's that bastard Andrew isn't it? " He puts his hand to his mouth. " I'm sorry, I didn't mean that, let me try again. " He thinks for a second before rephrasing. " It's that cunt Andrew isn't it? "

Theo laughs heartily. " How did you know? I'm sure I gave you no clues. "

Callum , putting his arm around him, leads him to the white leather sofas set against a black and white, grey and red Piet Mondrian style wall, hidden away under the majestic winding spiral staircase.

" It's fine, it's just something I'm dealing with.. It's a new realisation and I really don't want to talk about it. "

" Sure, and I'm straight as a nail. "

" Okay, so I do want to talk about it. " He brings the drink to his mouth. He fidgets in his seat, trying to formulate into words the conclusion that he had come to in the cafe.

" The thing is, I realise now that Andrew and I are not progressing in the relationship, we have become lazy. Well, *he* became lazy I should say. It's not exciting anymore. It's just formulaic. Or, maybe it always has been. We're just two people who fuck, nothing more, nothing less. "

" Well, " He says leaning over Theo to get some marinated olives from the table. " Is the sex at least any good? "

" Trust you. " Theo sighs.

" What does that mean? Trust you? "

" Of all the things you could have said, you focus on the fucking. " He says nudging Callum in the ribs. " Bet you'll be asking me how long he lasts for in a minute! "

Callum waits with his hands open towards Theo.

" Oh my god, *you want to know, don't you?* " He takes another sip of the potent drink, as the cherry note fills his palette. " Well, it's not pretty, no longer than three to five minutes, tops. "

" What? You're kidding me, I've taken shits that last last longer than that! "

" I know, I know, but however brief it is, give him his due, he does know what he's doing when he's doing it. It's just that it's not long enough. It's like eating those individual pots of Haagen Daaz. You can't believe how good it feel when it's inside you, and before you know it, you're scraping the bottom of the tub to get every last drop of satisfaction, to no avail. "

" One question: How do you make yourself cum with such a.. How do I put it.... tight schedule? "

" Oh That part's easy. Two words..Taye Diggs. "

" Amen Theo, amen "

The two continue to talk over drinks as the live band bursts into life, the Cuban flavoured drink filling their mouths and the bands Latin music resounding in their ears. Theo confides in Callum about his decision to talk to Andrew about his feelings, and in return Callum continues to shock Theo with his latest conquests. It was just like old times again. They were just having their third tequila shot of the night when the two were interrupted.

" Excuse me. " A very masculine voice resonates from above. The man that stands towering above them was smiling confidently with warmth. " I don't usually do this, but I saw you when you came in and I can't keep my eyes off you. Do you have any idea how sexy you are when you smile? "

The two friends look at each-other unable to say anything.

The stranger, sensing that although it was the right place, clearly wasn't the right time, pulls a pen from his leather jacket pocket and starts to write on a bar receipt. " Once again, please accept my apologies for my rudeness for interrupting you both in what appears to be a very deep and meaningful conversation. I just could not let the opportunity pass me by to let you know how stunning you are. " He extends the piece of paper, scribbled with his number, as Callum snatches it from him quickly.

" Why thank you baby, I will be sure to call you tomorrow, but you are correct we are in the middle of something. I'm trying to get my friend to realise his relationship is a total train wreck, so why don't you just go on home and wait eagerly by the phone for my call. " He looks at Theo, rolls his eyes and whispers. " I'm *so* sorry T, this is always happening to me, now where were we? "

The stranger, looking bewildered, interrupts again. " I think you misunderstood - "

Callum lifts his finger towards the stranger, stopping him in his tracks.

" No, I think you misunderstood me honey. Yes, I see you looking sexed up in your black leather jacket, white shirt, black metallic effect tie and leather trousers, looking like you just stepped out of the latest Usher video, but you are just going to have to wait this one out, ok? " Callum continues to shake his head whilst Theo looks on bemused.

The stranger disappears for a moment, then returns, this time with a drinks receipt, the same number scribbled on the back and gives it to Theo.

" Please! Tell me you did not just give the same digits to my friend? Bitch, you do realise I am *still* here?? "

He turns to Theo, ignoring Callum. " Please tell your ego inflated friend, that this number was *never* intended for him. It was intended for you, sweetness. "

Callum's mouth drops to the floor, speechless.

The man turns back towards a now, gobsmacked Callum.

" Believe me, my coffee is already strong and black enough as it is, I prefer milk or cream with mine. " He turns back towards Theo and smiles seductively before walking away saying. " Call me, I'd love to get to know the man behind the smile. "

" I knew! " Callum shouted after him. " I *knew* it was my friend you were interested in and *not* me!"

Some of the men sat nearby, who had heard the whole conversation, try to stifle their laughter unsuccessfully.

" It's just something me and my buddy do when were out! Livens up the evening don't you think!? " The stranger, walking back to his friends shakes his head in disbelief.

Theo, knowing the awkwardness that Callum would be feeling, reaches out his hand and lays it over his. " So, have I told you I'm working on some new material? "

" No! That's so great baby! It's been so long since you have written any new stuff! I was beginning to think your ideas had all dried up. " He pauses and points in the direction of the stranger who had now rejoined his friends. " Like that guy's sex life if he continues to pull that kind of shit every time he likes someone. "

Theo smiles and looks him directly in the eyes. " Oh, come on Callum. You know if it had been you that he was interested in, you would already be doing your ass exercises on this very seat in preparation. "

" He wishes. " He says shooting him another glare. " So what's the new stuff about? "

" A mixture of things really. " He says stroking his face. " Some are based on reflection of previous relationships that I've had, but the ones that I am really excited about are from observing strangers. " He relaxes back in his chair. " A couple of them came from listening to conversations in coffee shops between mothers and daughters, or in pubs between workmates. " He takes another sip before sitting up enthusiastically. " Oh, and then there was the thing that happened last weekend. I was on the train travelling to see my parents and the carriage was really quiet. There was a woman a few seats in front, talking on her phone to what I can only assume was one of her girlfriends. She was talking about this guy she had recently met and how they had spent this incredible time together and how romantic it had been and how she couldn't wait to see him again. "

" Wont last, bet you. " Callum says knocking back his drink.

" Well, it's funny you say that, because a few moments later, the conversation took a complete u-turn when she had an incoming call. She asked her friend if she could call her back because it was the guy she was seeing who was on the other line. She said her goodbyes excitedly and answered the call. " He takes a deep breath and exhales slowly. " The call started off well with laughter and a few giggles, which then quickly turned to concern and anxiety. Before you know it, her voice was breaking more with each word that was coming out of her mouth. " Theo puts his hand to his chin and shakes his head as he recollects. " He was finishing with her. All I could think about were two things: How much I wanted to give her a big hug and tell her it was going to be okay, and how, even I would have not seen it coming. "

" What are you talking about T? What do you mean, ' even I wouldn't have seen it coming ' you weren't even there? "

" I know, but what I mean is, listening to the conversation she was having, it sounded like her weekend had been ripped straight out of an old forties romance movie. You know, hearts and flowers, and big romantic gestures. I never imagined it turning into a five hundred days of summer scenario. "

" Okkkayy.. " Says Callum scanning the room briefly for men.

" You clearly haven't seen it then, otherwise you would know exactly how heartbreaking it was to watch these two people with two completely different perceptions of their relationship. One convinced that this was the love of his life the other just treading water. "

" Well, if it's helping you to write music again, that's all that matters babe.. because...I have some news for you. There's this guy that I have recently met- "

" Fucked, you mean. " Theo says, annoyed at Callum's usual disregard for anything emotional.

" Actually, not this time. Of course I tried, but even I know he is totally out of my league. "

" Wow! I never in a million years thought that I would ever hear you do that! " Theo puts his hand strong to his chest.

" What? " He says.

" Be so self deprecating, it doesn't suit you. "

" Oh, you mean in the same way that those jeans don't go with those shoes. " Callum chirps acidly.

" Anyway.. you were saying, you met this guy who you didn't fuck.. "

" Well, the last guy I *was* fucking is friends with this hot shot producer and we all met up for a drink and he's having an open audition for a new artist that he wants to sign to his label. It's no big secret in the industry that he is having this event, but I made sure that I talked you up to him, and told him to look out for Theo Morrison. "

" That's so great! I really do appreciate it hun. " He says leaning over to hug him. " When is it? "

Callum's phone starts to ring. He glances at the screen display and his face lights up. " I have to get this babe, I won't be long, back in a mo. "

Theo, knowing him like he did, knew that that would be his latest hook up on the phone, and that when he returned he would make a poor excuse and disappear. He reaches into his coat pocket to get some money for another drink, and instead, pulls out the card that the stranger had given him. He takes a look at the name on the card. Kez.

Wonder if it's short for anything? ' He thinks to himself. ' Keith, or Ken or maybe Kelvin. More to the point, why do I care what his name is? I mean no matter how shit my relationship feels right now, I definitely shouldn't be focusing on other men or what their name could potentially be. Although he is insanely hot and he smelt incredible. '

Callum's hand being placed on Theo's shoulder stops him mid-thought.

" Really sorry T, going to have to cut the night short. Something's turned up that I *really* can't get out of. I would tell you but it's long. "

" Long, is it? " Theo nods knowingly. " That's fine babe but before you go, the audition date, location? "

" Of course, shit! Let me text you it tomorrow. That's the one thing I didn't take a note of. " He leans down and kisses him on the cheek. " See you soon love. Oh and by the way, *he's* on his way over. " He says winking as he disappears.

" Who!? " He shouts after him.

"I think he means me. " Kez says putting his hand on his shoulder in exactly the same position where

Callum had put it moments before, but this time squeezing with more strength.

Theo turns around to see Kez, only this time he was sat down next to him, his strikingly handsome look now fully apparent. His skin, a mix of dark caramel and sienna appears to shimmer in the club. His hair, a polished fade ,complements his expensive black italian leather jacket. His worked out muscular body seems to shape to his silk white shirt, and his erect nipples Theo can't help but focus on.

He grins widely. " Hey, I'm Kez, but I'm guessing you know that already considering that you are holding the receipt I gave you with my name on. " He reaches out his left hand to shake.

" Hi, I'm Theo, but I'm alrea- "

" Really nice to meet you Theo. Can I get you something else to drink? " He says continuing to shake his hand warmly.

" That's really nice of you, and believe me I am flattered, because here you are, this unbelievably attractive man wanting to buy me a drink, and I would, but as I was saying I'm tak- "

" Come on Theo, I have a couple of Smokey Manhattan's back at my table with no one to drink it with. You wouldn't let me drink by myself would you? " He leans into Theo, his head tilted, eyes like Maltesers , willing him.

" I'm taken Kez. " He says firmly. " If there's one thing about me that will always remain true is, *I don't lie..* I'm taken."

" I know, " He says, continuing to smile, " remember your friend inadvertently gave me that information earlier when I first came over. "

" So, if you know this, *why* are you still pursuing me, huh? " He says bluntly.

Kez reaches in front of Theo and grabs the bowl of olives. " I have a good feeling. Call it a hunch, or intuition, or whatever, but there's something special about you and you are clearly not happy with the guy you are with, so why wouldn't I? I would be honoured to be the guy that makes you smile again. "

" Yes, you are right, I haven't been happy with him for quite a while, and yes, he may or may not be right for me, *but* under no circumstances would I cheat whilst I'm still with him. " Theo stands up to leave, extending his hand to shake Kez's. " So, I will say goodnight and tell you it has been genuinely nice to meet you because it has, and that I hope you find what you're looking for tonight. "

Kez takes his hand and turns it palm down, brings it close to his lips and kisses tenderly. " I already did Theo. "

Surprised by the man's overt display of affection, he doesn't say a word, but just smiles awkwardly and walks back out into the night and makes his way to Hanover Street.

Theo arrives at Andrew's expensive Mayfair flat, situated in between the Thai and Japanese restaurants on the corner of Princes Street, flustered, his heart beating furiously. He takes a moment to prepare himself for the conversation ahead. He thinks about all the things that Andrew could potentially say or do to convince him that there is nothing to discuss. *He could laugh it off, change the subject, or try to guilt me into avoiding the issues. He could even attempt to pacify me with sex, but whatever happens when I walk through the door, I knows that this time I have to be strong, I have to be prepared.* He looks his watch as he stands outside the white door, . ' *That's funny. It's one o clock in the morning and his bedroom light is on? On a work night he is always in bed by eleven, eleven thirty at the latest.* He fumbles for the correct key on the chain and carefully inserts. *'Perhaps he's having trouble sleeping... he has been stressed recently. The extra workload he's had to undertake since his co worker Paul decided to develop an unconvincing chronic back condition has meant he hasn't been home most nights before nine. Yes, that must be it.* He closes the door quietly behind him so as not to disturb what little sleep he may or may not be having.

He heads to the warmly lit kitchen, takes a glass from the overhead glass cabinet, and pours himself some wine from the half opened bottle of rose left on the work top. He presses his hand firmly on the cold black granite and pushes hard from his shoulder down to his finger tips. *Perhaps I should wait until the morning. It can wait.... no it can't. He needs to know how unfulfilled I am. You never know he might be feeling exactly the same way but just too scared to say anything..shit.. why is this so hard to see myself walking up the stairs and just telling him?* He releases his grip on the smooth surface, turns around and steadies the back of his head on the cupboard and stares at the draining board. A faint moan of restlessness coming from the direction of the hallway brakes his concentration temporarily. *He must be awake, I need to do this now.* With one final swig, he hastily swallows the remainder of the wine and puts it down next to the other two glasses on the draining board.

" Two glasses? " He says to himself faintly.

He takes a closer look and stops dead.

Hang on, they still have remnants of red wine left in them! He feels the blood draining from his face and the muscles in his body tightening.

Someone else was here tonight, and it definitely wasn't any of his friends because they don't ever drink wine...

The stifled groan he had heard earlier, now returns growing louder and more intense as if to taunt him.

Someone else is still here!

Theo follows the noise to the bottom of the stairs and starts to climb as quietly as possible, all the while desperately trying to think of a innocent explanation for the groaning. He reaches the top of the landing, his heart pounding so loud. He wonders how Andrew has not heard him approaching. His hand hovers over the handle unable to open the door for fear of seeing the inevitable. Andrew deep inside another man. He waits, intently listening for the next moan. Nothing.

I must be going crazy! There's no one else here. If there was, I would have heard someone by now. I need to get out of here, this just proves this can wait until tomorrow, I'm losing my mind! Andrew wouldn't cheat.

Just as he pulls his hand away, the handle thrusts downwards and the door opens to reveal a woman, a naked woman.

CHAPTER 3

" So, let me get this straight, you only just found this out now? " Maria says handing Amelia a face wipe.

" Yes sis, and I probably know what you're thinking too..how could I not know? " She says, her tanned skin glowing from the light coming from the vanilla scented candle in the wooden pillar holder in the centre of the table.

" Well, actually yes! I would be lying if I said it hadn't crossed my mind ! " Her fingers touching her temples in despair before letting them drop to her side. " I mean, how does someone not find out something as important as *this*? You're two weeks *today* away from your wedding day Ame! "

" Really? I had no idea! Thank you so much for pointing that out! I knew there was something important coming up that I had to do! " She says sarcastically, still managing to look impossibly beautiful through torrents of tears.

Maria raises her hands back to her head, takes a deep breath and exhales slowly. " Okay, I deserved that, I'm sorry. I'm supposed to be supporting you here. The thing is, and you probably won't believe me when I tell you this, but I'm having the exact opposite problem to you at the moment. " She says gesturing, her little finger extended.

" No! " Amelia gasps with the news of her sisters unfortunate revelation.

" Yes, but, I digress, this isn't about me. " Her fore finger and middle finger resting on her bottom lip. " So, how big exactly is he? I mean bigger than you are used to, or porn star big? "

She fingers her hand through her hair before speaking. " Porn star big.. and then some.. and *then* airbrushed. "

" Oh wow! " Maria says looking at her sisters crotch without thinking. " I actually don't know what to say. " She crosses her legs empathetically. " I *do* have some very good pelvic floor muscle exercises you can do though that will help you after? " She looks deep into her sisters eyes. " Ame.. what are you going to do? It's not like you're trying to fit the contents of a three bedroom house into the space of a one bedroom flat, cos that's do-able. " Her hand drunkenly swaying her glass of Merlot from side to side as she continues. " This is basic biology. If it doesn't fit, it doesn't fit. "

" Don't you think I know this! " She finishes her glass in one unceremonious gulp. " I either finish with him or start wearing incontinence pants ! " Amelia states, her smile halfhearted.

" So, does he know? Have you given him any clue? "

" Nope, he's oblivious. You know what men are like! Once they get aroused, you can tell them anything and they won't be listening. " She says refilling her glass with wine. " I could tell him I'm his long lost sister halfway through sex and he would still continue to do me! The problem is.. I love him, and you know me, I don't say this stuff lightly. I really love him. What am I going to do Maria? "

" Well, let's think about this. " Maria reaches out a hand and steadies it on her sisters tension filled shoulder. " We know that he loves you too. " She says pausing, " Let's face it, he wouldn't be taking on a child from a previous relationship unless he did. " She rationalises, " So, if sex is important to him, then you are going to have to find a way around it. " She eases herself off the cream corner sofa and paces back and forth behind Amelia.

" Have you thought about concentrating on giving him oral sex instead? "

" Maria, sis, whilst I appreciate you trying to help me, *really* think about it. If *that* part of me has a problem with it, don't you think my throat has *exactly* the same issue! "

" Shit, you're right! I'm sorry Ame, I'm not thinking straight. I'm pretty drunk right now. Which, believe me, is a good thing, because there is no way in the world I would be able to have a conversation like this with you, my little sister, without having copious amounts of alcohol inside me. " She walks into the kitchen and returns to the living room with an ample two tone wooden bowl filled with crisps. " I have to ask again Ame, how did you not know?! "

Amelia, struggling to find the words, finally blurts out.

" *Because we hadn't even seen each other naked up until last Tuesday.* "

" What?? Seriously? " Her voice registering an octave higher than usual. " Are you telling me you hadn't even had *SEX?!* Surely everyone knows in this day and age, you *have* to try before you buy? "

" No! " Her hand extends expressively. " We hadn't had sex! We hadn't done the nasty, we hadn't bumped uglies, we hadn't screwed, porked, fucked, whatever you want to call it, we *hadn't! okay!* "

" Okay.. " Maria says calmly, sensing the urgency in her sisters voice.

" At the time we started seeing each other, we both decided on celibacy, and *at the time*, it seemed like a pretty great idea. "

" Really sis? Seems like a pretty crazy idea to me. "

" Well, with my track record with men, it seemed sensible. We both realised that when you remove sex from the table, there's no confusing the strengths or weaknesses in the relationship. "

" Right.. " Maria says, unconvinced.

" What I mean is: Say for instance you have an argument. " She says grabbing a handful of crisps. " And talking it through doesn't resolve anything.. "

" Okay. " Maria says listening intently.

," You will always have sex to fall back on to make everything alright again, agreed? "

" True. " She says nodding resignedly. " Very true. "

" Now, if you take sex out of the equation, what you're left with, is two people who are forced to be open, honest, and really willing to communicate with each other. "

" Sis, you're starting to sound like mum. " Maria says flatly.

Amelia answers frostily. " Well it doesn't matter anymore anyhow! It was working brilliantly, until I decided to have that bloody sherry!! "

" Sherry? I didn't even know you kept alcohol in the house ever since you had Leigh. " She refills her sisters glass. " You told me you' d made a conscience decision to make sure it was not in the flat after you watched that episode of Trisha when she talked about the dangers of alcoholic substances being left in the house."

" You're right, I don't normally keep alcohol in the house. That day was different though. It was the night of one of Tom's work functions. You know me, I hate them and would normally try and get out of it, but I had just had a particularly crappy day fighting with my next door neighbour, who, up until then, had had no problem with me, whatsoever. "

" So, what changed? " She quizzes. " Jen has always seemed so lovely. Oh, and her son too, what's his name? "

" Simon. "

" That's it, Simon, what a cute child. "

" Well, that's what I thought too. " She says with sass. " Turns out not so adorable after all. Unless you find it ' cute ' to see a seven year old, running around the garden with a particularly lifelike toy gun, screaming ' Die fucker! ' at the top of his voice! "

" Wow, So Simon's vocabulary has dropped to the gutter. " Maria says smirking.

" I know! Right? Well, as you can imagine, I felt that it was important to let his mum know, since she always seemed so well spoken and presentable. "

" As you would. " She takes a crisp from the bowl and leans in, listening. " I would have done the same thing, if I had friends that had children. "

" So, I get to her door and call out...no answer. The door was ajar, so I let myself in. When I walked through the door into her hallway, I soon learned where Simon had picked up his new found colourful language, since *his mum* was using it, to scream at the television programme she was watching! " She waits for her sister to react. " The minute she saw me she turned so red! I thought it was due to the embarrassment she should have been feeling from being caught out. I couldn't have been more wrong. " She leans in close to her sister. " She was turning red with anger at *me* for disturbing her mid rant! "

Maria covers her mouth in shock. " That must have been awkward. "

" *She* shouted obscenities at me, *I* shouted them back, and before you know it, we're enemies all within the space of a few minutes. "

" Ouch! " Maria mouths whilst walking across to the muted silver I Pod speaker dock to play some background music.

" Oh, and the best part of the story, is that in the middle of this shouting match Simon had walked back into the living room, and was aiming the gun at me screaming . ' My mum never liked you anyway! ' Followed by the obligatory, ' Die Fucker! ' sentence he has grown so attached to. Charming huh? "

" Just goes to show, you think you know someone. "

" Exactly! Anyway, after everything that had happened, when Tom walked in from work, I had already raided the cupboard for the bottle of cooking sherry I had bought for making christmas puddings. He mentioned the works do and I was sold. "

" It all becomes clear now. " Maria nods.

" Believe me, nothing was clear on that night. Well, except the size of his cock. Oh, and the worst thing about it, is that when it was over, he told me that he knew I was the right girl for him because before me, *nobody had been able to accommodate him !!!!* " She throws her hands up in despair. " Now he tells me!! "

" Looks like all that honest and open communication didn't extend to the size of his cock then. "

" Very funny! Whichever way I look at it, I don't know what to do, and then to confuse things.. Actually forget it.. " Amelia looks away into the kitchen.

" There's more?? " She says expressively. " What could possibly be more? "

" No really, forget it, it's fine. It was a mistake and I just want to block it out. Pretend it didn't happen anyway. "

Maria sits, waiting for her sister to finish the story, despite her evident insistence to refuse disclosure of any details. " What did you do Ame? Remember, you came to me tonight, which already tells me that you had every intention of telling me the *whole* story. So, spill. "

" I hate you. You know that, right?? " She breathes in deeply.

" But, you're right. I just don't know how to say the words without feeling utterly disgusted by myself Maria. "

" Well, let me help you out sis. " She says leaning into her, her hand gently touching her knee. " You pretty much told me what you did, just by that look on your face as the words came out of your mouth. So what's his name? "

Amelia's face changes from immediate surprise to realisation of the obviousness of the situation. " It's Jeff. "

" Amelia, no! There's a reason why ex's are ex's and why they should stay that way! " She lowers her voice, remembering that her sister already felt bad. " So, why Jeff? Or is it as simple as Jeff's dick doesn't destroy you? "

Amelia's hand covers her face in shame. " Okay, I have now gone from hating you to *despising* you, how are you doing this? Am I that see through?? "

Maria reaches over and squeezes her hand. " No, not at all hun, you just have to know that when you get to thirty, everything and anything is possible, believe me. So when did this happen? "

" It was a few weeks ago, I bumped into him at the Icebar just off Regent Street on a girls night out. I had already shared a punch bowl of Tinsel Town and way too many Vanilla and Apricot Sours before I realised he was in the bar. He looked different, *so* different that I almost didn't recognise him sis. " She looks up to her left, recalling the memory. " He had this look about him, I can't quite describe it or put my finger on it, but, it was a maturity. Plus a definite improvement in taste of clothes. " She sighs at the recollection of all of the good memories they had made at the beginning of their relationship.

" Oh, and he got rid of that dreadful goatee, you know the one that only Craig David can get away with. "

" Oh yes, the goatee. How could I forget that. "

" Anyway, It happened, I slept with him. End of. " She says resolutely. " It felt great during, then I felt like shit in the morning. So, help me hun? What do I do? I can't keep avoiding the situation. " She says sitting forward. " I swear it knows. "

" It?? " Maria says, mystified.

" His dick!! It knows! It knows it's so big. It's like the kid in school that has rich parents. "

" What? You've lost me now. "

" You know? When a kid knows its privileged. He or she knows they're bigger, better or has more money than everyone else. "

" Oh, I see, I think. " Maria says smiling. " There' s only one thing you can do. You just have to be honest with him. Tell him he is larger than most. Oh, and don't tell him he' s too big because he wont believe you. Most guys are so incredibly insecure about the size of their appendage that he'll think you are taking the piss out of him. Then you need to find new positions, new angles, and without a doubt, new lubrication. "

Suddenly, Maria's phone ringing, disturbs her mid thought. She checks to see who it is. *It's Theo. I'll let it go to voicemail, he's probably just calling to check the outcome of tonight.*

" If you need to get that, I understand sis. "

She places her phone back into her bag. " It's only Theo, he usually calls me to let me know he's back home safe. So, back to you? Any thoughts? "

Amelia thinks for a second." Maybe it's time for me to move on. "

This was not the first time that Amelia had felt this way because of a man. In fact, the first time that she had uttered the very same sentence was just under a year ago. It had been a decision that she had not taken lightly, but nonetheless, one that she had felt necessary. To make matters worse though , it wasn't just over any man, it had been over Maria's man, Marcus.

It had been a chance meeting one night in September when Amelia had first met him. Maria had uncharacteristically double booked herself for dinner plans, and it was only when she answered the knock at her door to see both her boyfriend, Marcus and Amelia standing in front of her, that it clicked. Amelia , realising what had happened from the surprised look on her sisters face, graciously offered to leave. Before Maria could thank her sister for understanding , Marcus had ushered her in to the apartment, saying that he didn't mind the extra person and that it was a great opportunity to meet his potential sister in law. Within moments, the three of them were drinking Margarita's, eating the tapas Maria had prepared, and talking as if they had been friends for years.

Weeks passed by and before they knew it, it had become a regular Wednesday night thing. They would get together, talk, cook and watch late night chat shows and laugh at the absurdity of the lives the guests led. However, their comfortable existence did not last, and when Maria had to leave for Spain for six months because of work, the dynamics rapidly changed.

Marcus had continued to ask Amelia to come over as before, since he could see no reason to stop the tradition of the Wednesday nights, just because Maria wasn't there. After all, he had no other plans and he liked Amelia's company.

Even though she had felt strange at first at his proposition, Amelia soon rationalised her concerns and continued to see him, as she also enjoyed his company whether Maria was there or not.

For the first few weeks, everything seemed comfortable, enjoyable, and relaxed, albeit after an initial awkward first time. It was about two months in when she sensed the change in him. He had shifted from talking about Maria with fondness, to arguing with her on Skype when she had to cut their time together, short. The arguments became more frequent, and she could sense the resentment in his voice whenever he talked about her. He would complain about her over dinner, followed by awkward silences, followed by insincere apologies for his inappropriate outbursts in front of her.

His focus became less and less orientated towards her and more towards Amelia. He started to make more of an effort in his appearance at dinner. Gone were the jogging trousers, and in place of them designer jeans and shirts, and the generic aftershave now upgraded to Armani and Davidoff colognes.

Instead of the usual dinner served on a tray, he would light candles at the dining room table for them. At first, she would tell herself not to read anything into it, and to not be so melodramatic. She would shrug the feeling off every time it resurfaced, choosing to believe he would never want to stray from her sister, until *that* day. The day that changed everything. She had arrived at the apartment as usual, her hand about to press the door bell. Just before she did, she had heard a glass smash from within the apartment.

For a second she thought to leave, to turn and to go in case something was wrong, but she felt bad to go without checking on him. She pressed the bell lightly and waited for him to open the door. Just before he opened the door she had heard him quietly sobbing, the urgency in his voice, intense. His face lightened slightly upon seeing her as he flung his arms around her. The unusual display of affection both surprised and worried her. He had seemed very different. A fire in him was burning beneath his skin, surfacing through his eyes.

"We're over." He sobbed uncontrollably, " She left me." His body collapsed into her momentarily before strengthening again.

"Oh my god! I'm so sorry Marcus. " Her thoughts raced between her sister and him. " Is there anything I can do? "

His hands grasped her arms more forcefully. His face, at once, so suddenly contorted. " *Why? Why would you care?! If your sister didn't care, why the fuck would you?!* " He released her from his grip, turning his back on her. " Did you know? "

Amelia stood, glued to the floor. " Of course I didn't know, do you honestly think I would be here if I knew she was going to do this? "

He walked to the fridge, grabbed a beer, opened it, and knocked it back in one go, before looking at Amelia sternly.

" Did she tell you we hadn't had sex for months? All the travelling with her fucking new job took care of that. "

Amelia, still anchored firmly in one spot, her voice trembling slightly as she spoke." I don't know what to say Marcus, I .. I'm so sorry. As you know, Maria and I have never been that close, up until we all met that night. We're not the kind of people who share stories or talk in great detail about what is going on in each others lives. I promise you I didn't know. "

" Whatever, " He slurred picking up another beer before slumping to the floor. " *It doesn't matter now, it's over. I should have known your fucking sister was no good!* "

Amelia , paralysed in fear from this new frightening, aggressive side she was seeing in him, looked in the direction of the door. " Look, I should go, I ...I'm really sorry, I'll call you later Marcus. "

She waited for a moment for him to speak, the room, now deathly silent. She looked at the crumpled mess on the floor that was Marcus, turned her back on him, and edged slowly towards the door. She felt the cold metallic sensation in her hand as she turned the door knob.

Nothing happened , the door didn't move.

It was then that she felt the warm, sickly sweet breath on the back of her neck, and the sensation that someone was towering behind her. She glanced back to see it was Marcus holding the door closed.

" Why ? Why are you trying to leave as well?! What is wrong with you fucking Martinez sisters? I know you kind of look like her, but do you have to be a bitch like her too ?? " His hand thumping the door so hard it resonated throughout the flat.

" Look, Marcus, you are a good man, but in case there is any doubt in your mind, you are scaring the shit out of me right now! I'll call you tomorrow? Okay? " She said as assertively as she could, though deep inside she was petrified of the potential, the potential of what he could do to her.

" You're not going anywhere Amelia, you need to show me that you understand, that you care, that you get what I'm going through! " He stumbled heavily across the floor, his arm now locked around her waist, pulling her back into the kitchen.

Tears welled up in her eyes, half from fear and half from pure determination. She could see where this was leading, she could see exactly where this was going in vivid detail. She refused to be a victim, refused to be another statistic. She wouldn't allow this to happen, not now, not ever.

He fumbled with his belt with his one free hand, eventually unfastening it. His jeans dropped to the floor to reveal the shape of his erect penis beneath his underwear. He sneered , disrespectfully, pushing her head towards his groin. The tears streamed down her face as he forced her head onto his cock. He had grown so powerful that all the plans she had devised to escape him, soon seemed so futile. She told herself to bite, just bite as hard as she could and then run, but all she could think about was of the repercussions of her actions. Sure she could do some great damage, but he would catch her and he would be sure to beat her. In fact, he could actually *kill* her. The grip on her head from his hands tightened further, forcing himself further down her throat. She closed her eyes, so tightly, wishing, hoping that if she told herself this wasn't happening, then it wouldn't be. That she would wake up any moment now, drenched in sweat after the nightmare. She knew this was real though, the sensation of not being able to breathe, the inability to control herself from urging , and then finally the salty aftertaste as he ejaculated inside her mouth.

He slumped back, falling heavily onto the hard ceramic anthracite floor tiles, nearly knocking himself out. Amelia, dazed, disorientated and confused grabbed her bag and, after a few attempts , managed to pull herself up from the floor. She started to sob heavily again at the sight of her abuser laying on the floor. *How could he do this to me ? In all the time I've known him, there has never been a time, not even for a second that I have thought he would ever have done anything remotely violent. So barbaric, so inhumane.* She bent down close to him, and spat the remains of his seed onto his face in disgust. She turned and walked towards the door, stopped and shivered at the recollection of what had just happened. Then it dawned on her. *How am I going to tell my sister?! Perhaps she doesn't need to know, after all she's finished with him now? What happens if he tries to get her back though, now I've seen what he is capable of, I owe it to my sister to tell her, to warn her.* As the thoughts raced through her mind, she knew that no matter what she did or did not tell her sister, it would only push them further apart than they already were.

Two days and three bottles of Chardonnay later, she blurted it out to her sister after picking her up at the airport. She cried, Maria cried and they both apologised unnecessarily to each other for the experience that Amelia had endured.

The next day, still suffering with jet-lag, Maria had decided to confront Marcus. She chose her location wisely, and for her own safety, decided on a crowded bar. Naturally, as Amelia had anticipated, he denied every single thing. Instead fabricating a convincing and compelling version of the horrific turn of events in his favour. He told her how surprised he was at *her* advances towards him on the night he abused her. He told her that his injury came from Amelia pushing him over as she tried to mount him. In his version of events, *he* was the non consenting party, *he* was the victim, and that it was Amelia who's lust towards him was the culprit. He even broke down and cried in front of her. Maria was left filled with doubt. In her mind, even though the relationship had ended irreconcilably, she had lived with Marcus, and she too had never seen any violent tendencies in their relationship. Maria returned to Amelia at the end of the day to tell her everything that had happened at the bar, and even though at every step of the way she had supported her sisters version of the story, the niggling doubts never quite disappeared. Over the next few weeks the two sisters gradually spent less and less time together, making unconvincing excuses to cancel coffee days or shopping trips until they were barely in each other's lives. The distance spent apart became further confirmation that their own relationship was falling apart , dying until eventually dead, like Maria and Marcus's.

" Ame, it won't help anything! You leaving just means you're taking the issue to a different location. You've heard the phrase ' elephant in the room ', well, if you just up and move they'll be a fucking giraffe where that elephant's supposed to be! "

" Well, then you need to help me because I don't know what to do! "

The room falls quiet, then a faint beeping breaks the silence before a monotone is heard.

Maria was the first to speak. " What is that noise? It's not my phone, mine's off? "

Amelia scrambles for her phone. She empties the contents of her pockets, her bag and her jeans, onto the floor. She drops to the surface of the carpet for a closer look to try and find it amongst the lipsticks, notebook, and fake eyelashes.. nothing. She looks back at Maria, who is pointing at where Amelia has just been sat, her hand clasped over her mouth.

" What!? " She says picking up her phone at the same time as realising what Maria has just seen. The beep they had heard, was confirmation that someone was disconnecting the call, and the tone heard afterwards, had been the phone hanging up.

" *No, no, no* ! " Amelia shrieks. " *It says I have dialled Tom, and that the call was connected for the last fifteen*

minutes! "

" He might not have heard Hun, it's probably okay. Don't think the worst, honestly. I have sat on my phone a million times before. " Maria says shakily.

" Do you think? God, I really hope nothing.. " Then there was another beep, this time a shorter one. It was a notification of a text message.

" What does it say Ame? " Maria says, fearing the answer.

Ame slumps to the sofa, dropping the phone to the floor unable to speak.. Maria picks up the phone and reads the damning message.

' I heard everything. Everything.'

CHAPTER 4

" Maria, it's me... I don't.. I can't.... Shit! Shit! SHIT! "
Theo breathes unevenly, the emotion in his voice
clearly apparent. " I need to see you tomorrow, my
head's a mess, an absolute fucking mess! I can't even
believe what I've just seen..." The scent of the
woman's perfume still freshly fills his nostrils."
Andrew's a bastard, a fucking bastard! Are you free
tomorrow night? Please say yes? Anyway, give me a
call if you can make it Hun.. Bye.. "

He puts his phone on vibrate hoping that the next
person to ring him back will be Maria and *not*
Andrew. A familiar sounding voice interrupts his
thoughts, making him jump slightly.

" What can't you believe you have just seen Theo? "

Theo turns around in the direction of the voice, but
can barely make out the figure standing there.

" Who's there? " He strains to recognise the tall man
emerging from the shadows.

" Am I that forgettable, handsome ? " He says wryly.

The stranger walks forward, emerging from behind
the William Pitt statue in Hanover Square, to reveal
that it is Kez. His full black attire previously hiding
him from view.

" What the hell are you doing here!? Are you stalking
me? "

" No, why do you say that Theo? "

" Well, I may be upset and disoriented but I'm certainly not stupid! This place is at least fifteen minutes away from the restaurant I just met you at! "

Kez smiles openly, bemused by Theo's outburst. " I actually live just across the road. My building doesn't allow smoking so I usually come over here and spend some quality time with my thoughts, and my man right here. " He says pointing at the statue behind him.

Theo swears under his breath, unable to stop himself. " Look, I really can't do this right now. As you may or may not have gathered from the conversation I was just having, and the words that have *just* left my lips in the last few

minutes - "

" And lovely lips they are too, may I add Theo." Kez winks at him, moving closer.

" As I was saying, you would have gathered I'm having a pretty shitty... no, fucked up, day! Please can you just leave me alone to try and figure out what's going on in my head right now? " The phone vibrates in his pocket persistently. Theo takes the phone out. It's Andrew. He answers the phone roughly. He waits for a second as Andrew starts to speak.

" Oh, hang on, I'm a little bit confused right now, cos you are actually *speaking*. You see, I thought that when I answered the phone, all I would have heard would be background noise. " He waits for Andrew's inevitable bewilderment at his answer. " Why would I think that? Well, because I assume the reason you called me is because you must have sat on your phone and dialled my number *accidentally* because you can't honestly think for one fucking minute I would want to speak to you ever again by choice ?! Oh, and before you even try to tell me ' It's not what I think it is ', DONT! You clearly were not just *talking*, not unless you now talk naked with your friends. "

Theo paces back and forth listening to Andrew plead down the phone. He cuts in sporadically, his voice loud, yet stifled.

Kez stands by, watching, intrigued as to what has made him so angry and distressed. As he watches him, he finds himself mesmerised. He stops trying to listen in to the heated conversation, and instead funnels all of his attention on Theo himself. He can see that Theo is a little shorter than he had originally thought from seeing him in the bar, but this only endeared him further to him. At six foot two he liked to be taller than the guys he dated. He enjoyed the sensation of being protective of his partner, of being the strong man that guys like Theo craved. He watches as Theo frantically runs his hands through his dark brown dense hair, in between gesturing towards the phone expressively. So passionate, so emotionally available. His jeans fit him slightly too tight, even for his small frame, but they show cased a nicely rounded bottom. His red varsity jacket with black sleeves and white t-shirt suited his olive skin complexion, and his dark, yet caring eyes, burned with fire as he continued to chastise Andrew.

" Four words Andrew.. YOU..FUCKED..A...WOMAN!! and here's four more, NEVER FUCKING CALL AGAIN !!! Theo shouts before ending the call. He looks around, the whole time oblivious that Kez was still there.

"Come on! Why are you still here?! " Theo says exasperated.

" Just enjoying the view, Theo, just taking you all in. " He says smoothly.

" Well, don't! Do you have any idea, how much *that* worthless piece of shit, has taken from me?? " He yells jabbing his phone. " Aside from the countless loans that never got paid back, the time it took to prepare every meal to make sure it didn't have this in it, or that in it! I've had just about enough of guys like *you* thinking you can just take, take, take without asking! **Try giving back every once in a while!** "

" Oh trust me Theo, I only like to *give*, I *never* take. " He says, his words rich with double entendres.

Theo, livid from his conversation with Andrew, at first, misses the joke, but it isn't long before the penny drops and his guard begins to drop.

Theo takes one deep cleansing breath and massages his neck. " I'm sorry Kez, I really am. You definitely don't deserve this torrent of abuse from me. I'm honestly not normally like this. It's just that I've found out my boyfriend- "

" You mean the loser you were talking about with ' little miss thing ' in the club a few minutes ago...yep, go on? " He says mischievously.

" You know, Callum is really not that bad when you get to know him, he's got a heart of gold...but, yes, my boyfriend, the loser, the asshole, low life, cheating waste of space that he is, has been sleeping with - You know what, I can hardly bring myself to say this... with a girl. " He says, the words echoing through his brain. The statement so true, and yet so unreal.

Andrew has slept with a girl. He has actually slept with a girl, and evidently, he still is.

His brain, unable to process the information, repeats the same image of Andrew and her over and over again. Her at the door, probably going to the bathroom to wash the sex off of her, and him, laying in bed, looking content, fulfilled.

"You know what is so weird though? " He says, leaning against the metal fencing around the square.

"What's that's Theo? "

I don't even know who she is? I mean, you would think that if he had had the time to meet a girl, develop a friendship, then start fucking her, you would think at some point, I would have met her, right?"

" Theo- "

"Really?! *Where* did she come from? What is her name? More to the point, why do I even give a flying fuck what her name is? It's not going to change the fact that my so called gay boyfriend, is actually bisexual, or worse still, straight and has just been experimenting with *me* for the past few months. " He shakes his head, wishing he was back in the bar drinking himself to oblivion, trying to numb the pain." The least he could do is tell me why. Why her? Why has he chosen her over me? I don't want to sound like a bitter bitch but, she ain't no Mila Kunis. " He smiles slightly. " I know one thing though. It definitely can't be because of lack of sex, cos we had sex *all the time*, and damn good sex at that! " He paces the kerb back and forth. " I can tell you, I'm a very *accommodating* bottom!   Trust me, of all the short comings in our relationship, short cumming was *never* one of them! At least that's what he used to say when he was inside me! "

" Good to know Theo, good to know. " Kez says laughing.

" God.. " He hangs his head, shaking it left to right.

" What babe? "

" He has been *inside* her. "

' He weakens, beginning to lose balance. Kez, seeing him falter, rushes to him and catches him and within seconds has hopped the two of them over the railings into the park, sheltered from the hustle and bustle of the main street.

" What the fuck was that?! Are you some athlete or something, those railings are nearly as tall as you! "

"I work out.. A lot. Look, I know what you're going through Theo, and it's hard but- " He effortlessly puts Theo back on his feet before taking him to the park bench.

" I'm sorry Kez, but did you *just* say that you know what *I'm* going through? How on *earth* can you know what I'm going through? This isn't one of those situations where, I say something, then you come up with a similar thing to relate to, we bond, we feel closer, music starts playing in the background and we all live happily ever after! This is more like the twist in a really sick horror movie that you never saw coming! He is a gay man, who has only ever had gay sex with other gay men. So right about now, I doubt very much you could understand what is going on in my head, cos not even *I* can! "

" Theo, listen to me carefully. " He puts his strong hand firmly on his shoulder. " I *really know what you are going through..* "

" Really? You.. Know? " The hope in his voice was hard to contain.

" Unfortunately, yes. His name was Shaun. We dated for about a year. We met about five years ago. I was on a stag night in Brighton with some friends and he was out with his girls. He was cute, not unlike yourself, except he had a paler complexion. Our eyes met and within minutes I could hear laughter and giggling coming from the corner where he was sat. Everyone was smiling and waving, except one girl.

The way she looked at me was so venomous, but at the time I told myself *she* must be his closest friend and therefore very protective of him. I convinced myself that that was why she was giving me such a hard time,. How wrong was I, I should have known."

" I can relate to that though. Maria, my friend, is very protective of me, she would practically want a résumé and a full medical screening before she'll let me date a guy. " Theo says with humour, suddenly aware that Kez's hand was not just touching his shoulder, but was massaging it. It was so comforting to him,especially in light of the recent events, that he didn't object or resist. Instead, he just continues to listen to his dulcet tones as he continues to tell his story.

" Whenever Shaun and I were on a date, or arranging a trip away. There *she* was, creating a drama or an excuse for why she needed him to rescue her. I even tried to talk to her, one on one, to make her see that I was a good guy, and not some sleaze. "

Theo looked up at Kez briefly, acknowledging the statement.

" I know, I know, I can come across as a little bit arrogant. "

" A *little* bit arrogant? Honey, If your clothes could speak, even they wouldn't be sure if they were good enough for you! "

" Ha ha! Very funny! We both know I pull this off," He says grabbing the collar of his leather jacket. " Don't try and deny it. Seriously though, It's only because I know what I want, when I see it. I genuinely think you are beautiful Theo. Please don't ever think anything different. "

Theo, temporarily lost in the genuine compliment from Kez, interjects.

" So anyway, back to the story mister. You were talking about the bitch friend from hell. "

" Thanks for the reminder Theo. " He smiles warmly, and for the first time, his white teeth beam brightly at him.

He truly is stunning.There really is no denying it. He's like one of those pictures you look at and you see one thing, then you look again, and you see a different, more beautiful image materialising in front of you.

" So, she wasn't having any of it, she was determined to interfere. "

He shifts position from comforter to comforted as Theo sees the hurt in his eyes and puts his arm around him instead.

" Then, it finally happened on his birthday. I had this big surprise arranged for him. It involved dinner at Hakkasan followed by cocktails at Barrio Central in Soho, and then off to The Dorchester Hotel in central London for a marathon of sex. "

" Go on." Theo says neutrally, although inside, suitably impressed at the mammoth effort he had made for his boyfriend, and the mention of the word *marathon*.

"Well, I hadn't been able to get hold of him all day, and after leaving the eighth answer phone message, it was getting late, so I decided to go to his apartment and collect him. " He sighed, and put his hand on Theo' s. " That's when it happened. I had a spare key. I opened the door, walked into the kitchen, and there *she* was on the worktop riding my boyfriend's cock. "

" Oh my god! You really *do* know what I'm going through. " He says, realising how insensitive he had been.

" To this day, I don't know which part I found more shocking. The fact that it was a girl he was with, or that he was doing the fucking. He always told me he was one hundred percent passive, which is why we worked. Well, clearly he wasn't if he could be sticking his dick inside someone! I think the thing that hurt me the most though, was all the lies. I found out at a later date from her, when I was on a night out with the boys, that they had been fucking each other from the get go. In fact, they had been that way for as long as they'd known each other. "

" I hope you spiked her drink... with laxatives. " Theo says stroking Kez's hand. " Oh, and then emptied the girls toilets of all the toilet paper afterwards. " He says instantly. " I'm scared to ask, how long were you with the shit head? "

" Two years. Turns out *I* was the experiment. "

Theo looks him in the eyes. " I'm so sorry for being so confrontational about all this Andrew stuff. It's just that I honestly didn't see it coming. "

" Theo, come on now, I've only known you for a short time, but you *didn't* see it coming? A blind man could see that coming. Even a deaf man could hear the crash and burn of your relationship. You must be referring to the way it has come to an end, not the fact that it's over, no? "

" Okay smart ass, but there *was*, believe it or not, a part of me, however small, that thought that if I had managed to talk to him that we could have worked it out. That we could have talked it through. Not now though, *not ever*. Don't get me wrong, I love women, but there is never going to be a time in my life that I could be with a guy who is bi, or whatever he is. I need to know that the guy I'm with is only wanting to be inside a guy. I mean, how did I not see any signs? We used to watch television shows together, with plenty of beautiful women in them, and I never saw any stirrings in his trouser department. " Theo, lost in the moment, oblivious to everything, suddenly realises that tonight he had made a decision to stay at Andrew's place. He had felt so confident in his decision before the revelation, that he neglected to look at the time.

" Bugger! I've missed the last train back home to Balham! Shit, Kez I know it's a lot to ask, but can I get some money for a taxi back? I promise I'll pay you back. I was supposed to be staying with Andrew, and that's clearly not happening. God, I'm such an idiot. "

" You're not an idiot Theo, and sure, of course I can give you the money, don't worry about it."

The phone rings persistently in Theo's jacket.

Theo answers the phone aggressively. " *What the fuck do you want Andrew?!* " He waits impatiently. " *What? Let me get this straight, you want to talk?!* " He paces back and forth. " *Okay, you want to talk? So let's talk, so how was she? How did she feel as you were fucking her? How does it feel to have lied to us both on so many levels, cos I'm guessing that you haven't told her about me? How does it feel to know you have lost someone who was there for you every step of the way? Who supported you through thick and thin, who was unconditionally there for you no matter what?* " He waits , listening to Andrew beg and apologise insincerely over and over again. " *Look, I have to go now, I'm so happy for you and ... whatever her name is, but right now I have this strong sexy muscular black hunk, deep up inside my ass, fucking me the way you should have been doing all these years. He knows what rhythm is, he has way more style than you ever had, he is passionate and knows how to talk dirty with confidence, oh and by the way, he knows that holding a guy after he's fucked him, Is more important than rushing off to the eat the leftover Chinese from the night before!!* " He disconnect the phone.

Kez, hearing every word, stands and starts to applaud Theo. " Well, Theo my man, you have fire! Oh, and one heck of an imagination too. " He sits back on the park bench, and spreads his legs wide. " But one thing didn't sit with me."

"What's that Kez? " He says, his hands trembling with the adrenalin of the confrontation on the phone.

" Well, you said earlier on in the bar, that you don't lie about anything, but, you *just did.* "

" Oh come on Kez, seriously? You are going to deny me that? I need him to believe that. If I can make him feel one ounce of the betrayal I feel, then it's worth it !
"

" Oh, believe me I get it Theo. " He says, lowering his voice to a sexual drawl. " I'm just saying, I would hate for your record of not lying, to be compromised... Ever. " He smiles crookedly.

" Well, even if I wanted to take it back, it's too late now I can't, and I'm not even sure I want to, he deserves- " Kez interrupts him without using words, just his hand, beckoning him over.

" Awww, so naive, and so sweet. " He bites his lip seductively. " I think you're missing the point. In fact, I *know* you're missing the point." He widens his legs further.

" You're crazy! I'm not going to fuck you! "

" You're right Theo, *you're* not going to fuck me, *I'm* going to fuck you. " He says playfully.

" Okay, I've got to go, I have to find *somewhere* to stay! " Theo says, flustered, aware of the blood rushing to his dick. " *Don't* worry about the money, I'll find a way around it. I don't want to owe you anything, or give you any reason to get the wrong idea. " He starts to walk away but feels a breeze of air rush behind him, and the gentle, but firm hand of Kez pulling him back.

" Theo, you won't owe me anything, I don't expect anything, and truthfully, all I care about is that you get home safely. " Still behind Theo, He slips the money into his pocket with one hand, and puts the other one on his face. Cupping it softly, he leans in close to his ear. " All I care about is you mister. Just call me if you need me, ok? "

Theo, stunned by his generosity, his tenderness, and his kind natured words, momentarily forgets to exhale. The hot breath on the back of his neck, sends tingles up and down his body like electricity and sends his pulse racing like the first time he had realised he could sing. He feels his body tremble and his breathing become more vapid, but most of all he feels alive.

He keeps his body perfectly still, enjoying the sensation, and wanting it to never end. The eroticism of being in this position and the possibility of where this could lead was so powerful, so overwhelming. Kez, sensing the sexual tension, steps back from Theo and begins to edge away from him and just like a spell being broken, Theo let out the most urgent of breaths. He turns and rushes towards Kez, races past him and stops directly in front of him.

" What Theo? " He says startled by his sudden reappearance.

" I can't explain it and I don't even want to analyse it. I don't honestly know if I'm going to regret this tomorrow, but just kiss me. Please, just kiss me! "

Kez, without hesitation, wraps his strong arms around Theo's waist securing him in position, so he wouldn't be able to leave, even if he had wanted to. His face, previously saddened by Theo's rejection, now grins from ear to ear. Theo melts into his grip, staring into his deep wanting eyes, waiting for his evenly shaped lips to meet his. Kez, knowing now how much he wants him, teases him with the promise of a kiss, but pulls back, willing him to show exactly how much he wants his mouth, his tongue, his everything. Beads of sweat form on Theo's forehead and when he feels Kez's fast growing erection, he reaches down and rubs him eagerly. The sensation of Theo's hand on his dick, makes Kez moan with pleasure. His hand moves from Theo's waist to the back of his head, and his lips lock aggressively with his. Theo gasps for air as the warmth of Kez's lips, press down on his, and his tongue massages the inside of his mouth.

" My place is just around the corner ? Do you want to go? " Kez whispers into his ear before licking it slowly.

" No, I want you now, I need to feel you inside me."
Shocked by his own animalistic desire he feels
towards Kez , Theo stops temporarily.

" Don't stop Theo, that's so fucking hot! " Kez says
pulling him close, body to body.

" Oh god, you're driving me out of my mind! I want to
feel your big thick black cock so deep inside my tight
little white ass. "

Kez freezes temporarily, pleasantly surprised by
Theo's filth.

" Nice baby, such ugly talk from such a pretty little
mouth. " Egged on by his dirty talk, he unzips his
leather trousers and the tip of his huge dick emerges
from his Calvin Klein's. He turns Theo around and
thrusts and grinds his dick so hard against Theo's ass,
he almost penetrates him.

Theo, lips still intertwined, pulls down his jeans and
underwear and pushes his ass against him. " Shit! "

" What's wrong baby ? "

" I don't have any condoms, or lube for that matter.
You know, being involved with... Well, we stopped
using them. "

" No need to worry about that, I have both. " He
reaches into his pocket and pulls out a condom, rips it
open with his teeth and stretches it over himself and
applies the lube. " Oh, and let's not mention him now.
You have me baby, and I guarantee I'll do you better
than he ever did."

Theo, relishing the statement, takes the lube from him and starts to finger his own self. First with one finger, and then two, all the while fully aware this very act was turning Kez on effortlessly.

" You know I belong in your ass baby. I'm going to fuck you so good. " His dick visibly throbbing, pulsing, waiting for Theo to be ready to take him all the way inside.

He picks up Theo and carries him into the darkness of the surrounds trees, away from view. He holds him against the trunk of the thickest tree he could find with his powerful, sinewy arms, as Theo wraps his legs around his waist.

" Tell me how much you want me inside you Theo, how much you love the way I hold you, the way I kiss you. The way I make you feel how you've wanted for the longest time. I'm going to make you cum without you even having to touch yourself. " He says, his dick teasing Theo's hole.

" I can't remember the last time in my life that I've wanted someone so bad. " He pushes onto Kez's dick, slowly easing his ass onto his appendage, each inch feeling more intense and more pleasurable than the last, until he was all the way in. This stranger that Theo had resisted so ardently earlier in the night was now deep inside him. Filling him completely with his rhythmic strokes. It was true, Kez was fucking him better than Andrew ever had. In fact, better than any guy he had been with. He reacted to every facial expressions that Theo was making, as he thrust deeper and deeper, and angled himself accordingly, watching the pleasure wash over his face. At one point, he was so audible, Kez covered his mouth for fear of being caught by the diminishing general public making their way home in the early hours of the morning.

Theo, completely dominated by Kezs body, kisses him more urgent, his tongue probing furiously, his cock quickening and deepening with every thrust. He leans into Theo's ear and sticks his tongue in. His lips moving behind his ear, his stubble rubbing against his, causing friction. The stabbing sensation of him, hitting his prostate somewhere between pleasure and pain makes Theo lock his legs firmly around him. Every time Theo tries to reach his hand down to his own appendage, close to climax, Kez smiles and moves his hand back around his waist.

" I meant what I said, I'm going to make you cum without you doing a single thing." He says as he continues to press on Theo's now immensely stimulated erogenous zone whilst equally thrusting his tongue deep into his mouth.

Theo, feeling his legs give way with the intense pleasure, allows Kez to steady him. Sensing that he is close to orgasm Kez increases his speed of thrust until Theo let's out an uncontrollable, convulsing cry, and collapses into his arms.

Kez holds him tightly for a full minute before speaking.

" Are you okay? "

" I feel....I'm ..incredible." Theo sobs, tears seeping from his eyes, sweat dripping from every pore." Thank you."

" You don't have to thank me at all, the pleasure was all mine." He says grinning.

" No, I mean thank you for making sure I'm not a liar anymore." He smiles knowingly, gasping for air. " The truth is always important to me."

Kez holds him tightly in his arms as he carries a half naked Theo back to the steps leading to his place. " Lets get you to my bed and see if we can't make you tell the truth again and again."

CHAPTER 5

The clock in Maria's bedroom gently wakes her from her drunken, uneven sleep with its quiet yet persistent ticking. As her senses return, so does the recollection of the events of the previous night. She momentarily questions herself.

Could it have been a dream?

The weight of her sister, laying on top of her holding on so tightly, confirms that it was all too real. She remembers her sister crying, and the shock realisation that her boyfriend had heard everything on the phone, but there was something she couldn't quite bring to the front of her mind. Then it came to her. The unexpected phone call from Theo. She reaches across to her mobile phone and turns it on.

As she waits for her phone to start its lengthy initiation, her attention returns to her sister.

I wonder how she's going to cope? She looks down at her peacefully sleeping sibling. *She makes out she's so strong, so independent, but deep down she is still my little sister and still the same insecure girl she has always been.* Maria had picked up on Amelia's habit of over fussing with her hair when faced with high levels of stress. It was the same excessive attention that she had displayed last night as she had shown during the breakdown of their parents relationship. As her phone burst into life, the answer phone flashes. She listens to Theo's distressed message and without thinking, bolts upright, catapulting her sister halfway down the bed.

" Fuck Theo! What's that bastard done now !? " She shouts aloud to herself.

Amelia wakes, disorientated. " Maria! What.. *Why am I here?*What ... Oh my god *I think I'm going to be sick!* "

" Bathroom, on the left, second door, and please try not to get any on the walls like last time! I don't need a makeover in there, I like the colour perfectly as it is! " She calls out as her sister stumbles out the bedroom door.

In a few moments, Amelia can be heard emptying the contents of her stomach in between moans and retching. She stops briefly to speak.

" *Maria what the hell did we drink last night?!* Was it wine or balsamic vinegar, cos I swear that's all I can taste right now? "

" Actually, it was a wine that was on offer. Only three pounds down from nine, it was a bit of a bargain. "

" Well, if you ask me, if it was genuinely priced at nine, it would be a fine wine, but its priced at three, so it tastes like wee! " She quivers at the reoccurring taste in her mouth. " You know, sometimes there is a reason why a wine has that kind of reduction in price, and it's usually because it tastes like shit! Why did you give me that stuff? " She whines.

" I don't recall you complaining girl! You seemed more than happy to drink it last night, or was that someone else who was asking for the third bottle to be opened up because it was, as you put it ' awful nice ' ? "

" Really? Did I say that? Are you sure that I didn't say ' awful tripe? ' "

" I'm sorry, next time I'll be sure to get my best ' I fucked another man ' wine. From the vineyards of ' you brought it on yourself. ' I'm sure that will go down a treat. " She says under her breath.

" I heard that!!! " She says exasperated.

" Heard what Amelia? You really do need to get your ears sorted out, you're imagining things now. I didn't say a thing. " Maria says unconvincingly as she dials Theo. He answers nearly immediately.

" Theo! Are you okay, what happened ? Obviously it's Andrew but what did he do, or not do as the case seems to be with him these days ? "

" Um, can we talk about this tonight Hun? " He says extremely quiet. " I'm kind of in the middle of something right now. I'll explain later, say around eight thirty, my place? I'll make that Andalusian chicken you like so much. "

" That sounds amazing sweetness, I'll look forward to it, shall I bring some sherry this time? I've got some really authentic spanish stuff that will go perfectly with it, nana sent over some the other week ? " She says excitedly.

" Great, as long as it doesn't over shadow the bargain basement sherry I'm cooking it with. Right. Must go love, big kiss. " He says before abruptly ending the call.

Maria slouches back into her bed, the deep purple satin sheets covering her seductively. As she thinks about the events of the past day and night, Theo, with his manipulative boyfriend, and Amelia with her ' incompatibilities ', she can't help but realise that it's time for her to face up to her own romantic situation. Even though it had , up until now, made her feel better that she wasn't alone in experiencing the complications that love can bring, it didn't stop the nagging voice in the back of her head telling her that she has to finish with Chris. *It doesn't matter how he sticks it in, or where he sticks it. He can't satisfy me.* She pulls the covers over her head, frustrated. *I've almost forgotten what it feels like to climax. In fact, I think I've had more satisfaction from one square of a bar of Thornton's chocolate, than the collective times we have made love plus it's a whole lot less messier too!*

Her thoughts are interrupted by her sister slumping back onto the bed like an over fed family dog spanning the length of the foot of the bed.

" You look like shit Amelia. " She says with a sideways smirk.

" Really? Oh, I thought I was pulling off this look quite well. I call it ' throw up' couture. " She says dragging herself back up to her sisters side.

" Well, it would be a perfect look for you, don't get me wrong, but the strand of sick in your hair throws it all off. " Maria points at her fringe.

Amelia scrambles for her makeup mirror so she can locate the offending hair, before realising from the smile creeping across her sisters face, that she is teasing her.

" Just wanted to see you smile sis, there hasn't been much of that going on in your life from what I can tell. " Maria leans in to give her a hug. " So, about last night. You do remember what happened, don't you? " She reaches her hand to her forehead, recalling everything.

" Fuck! I genuinely had forgotten until you just said it then. I think between the cheap wine and the rude awakening this morning courtesy of yours truly, I really hadn't even processed why I was here in my sisters house in the first place. " Within seconds she hurtles towards the bathroom again for round two.

" Sorry Amelia, I should have waited until you had at least woken up, or had coffee or something. I'll get you something to settle your stomach. " Maria heads towards the kitchen and grabs an ice cold bottle of Mineral water from the fridge, adds some effervescent health salts and takes it to the bathroom where her sister lay on the floor, hair stuck to her face, ironically this time, with sick.

Maria hands her a towel and approaches the subject again, this time more tactfully. " Do you want me to call him? I can probably think of something to make up? I'm sure I can make it convincing. For one thing, he doesn't even know who I am, I've never met him so I can say it was me pulling some joke or stunt. It doesn't matter if he hates me, after all, I'm not screwing him. I can tell him that I've always hated you, and that I have been looking for the ideal way to ruin your life, I could be the super bitch jealous sister ! What do you think!?! "

Amelia looks her right in the eyes and smiles slightly at the irony. " We both know I have to tell him the truth. I have to admit everything. "

Maria reaches out her hand. " If it helps at all, I'm going to tell Chris too. We should do it together, like a double date. "

" Ooo, I like that idea. Or we could swap boyfriends, I'll have the small dick for a while, you have the massive one, everyone's happy. " Amelia says in jest.

" Now that's a solution ... For a guest on The Jeremy Kyle Show, that is. " Maria responds quickly, " Okay, I have to get showered and get off to work now Hun. I can see it being a late one, but please feel free to stay for as long as you like, and if you need some space from the inevitable fallout you know you're welcome here. There's a spare key behind the coffee tin in the

pantry and lots more of that wine from last night. "
She says giggling.

Amelia reaches out her hand as Maria vacates the
bed.

" Thank you sis, I really don't know what I would
have done without you last night, I know we haven't
really been close since- well. " She pauses. " You
know...... but I really am grateful. "

Maria's smile shifts from genuine warmth into one
tinged with sadness. " I know. " She squeezes her
hand to reassure her before going to the shower to
wash away the events of the night. Although she
knows it will take more than just a drunken night to
delete the past, it was a welcome beginning to the end
of the animosity she has felt towards her for years.

A rushed shower, and a unfulfilling bagel later, she
arrives at the office. She hadn't been due to work
today, but as per usual, she was playing catch up.
Knowing that her good natured work ethic was often
taken advantage of by her work colleagues, she did
not go to her usual office. Instead, she decides to head
to the first floor where she hoped to be uninterrupted
due to the executives being in a board meeting for the
entire day. It was a beautiful sunny day so she decides
to take her laptop to one of the offices with a stunning
view of the city below. She sits down with her Mocha
Latte, and takes a moment to herself before she
thinks about organising her desk to start work. It's

then that she sees him. Chris. Shocked at the sight of him so early, she wonders if he has read her mind for the past few hours and has somehow been drawn to her. She smiles at him warmly as he makes his way over to her.

" Hey there love, I missed you the other night. " He says eagerly.

" Okay, umm, about that, we need to talk." Her heartbeat racing so fast, her stomach turning, part from the admittedly cheap wine and part from the inevitable uncomfortable situation about to present itself.

" Talk as in, I've left the toilet seat up one too many times, or pissed on it again. "

" Look Chris- " She starts to formulate her words, but before she can finish, he stops her.

" Because, whatever it is, I can fix it. I can do better. " His voice urgent, waiting for her to condemn him with her next damning move.

" You can't fix this, Chris, it's not something that you've done wrong. " She looks into his eyes and frantically tries to think of a way out of the awkwardness.

" Of course it's me, if it wasn't me, then you would still want this. You would still want us." His eyes start to water. " *You would still want me.* "

Her mind races. *This is going to kill him. It would for any man. Why can't it be the other way around? It*

would be so much easier to tell him he's too big?
That's it! Of course! I can tell him it's too much.
The thing is Chris, is it really *isn't* your fault, it's just that you're too big! "

" What are you talking about ? Too big? " His tears drying. " I know I've gained a bit of weight recently, but everyone does around this time of year. You can't tell me your bum hasn't gained a little more bounce now? "

" Not big as in *fat*. Big as in your *dick*. I can't take it anymore!   Nice to know you think I have a fat ass though. "

" Stop trying to change the subject Maria. Where does this leave us? Can I not do something, or try something to make it better for you? This can't be over? I love you! " He says stroking her hand.

" Baby, it's not just your size, when you couple that with the fact that you are so highly sexed, I can't go on anymore! I'm constantly sore, or getting thrush! "

He looks at her, somewhat surprised at her confession, but doesn't argue. He doesn't resist, in fact he just smiles with melancholy. He reaches out and holds her tightly.

" I understand Maria. I can't say I'm not disappointed because I thought we had something good, but I equally don't want to cause you any pain. " He holds her tightly as she pretends to cry. " I have to say though, you're not the first person to tell me that so I know it's a problem. Friends? "

Bewildered , she could hardly believe he was buying it, *He is actually believing that he has a massive knob!' Is he blind? Does he not see the cocktail sausage hanging from his pelvis, I've seen new born baby boys with bigger dicks than his!*

" Of course! Thank you so much for understanding Chris, this decision didn't come easily, I've been agonising over it for a few weeks now. "

" You know, you could have told me, I hate to think of my gargantuan cock being at the brunt, literally, of the pain you've been going through. " He says half with concern and half with acute smugness.

She audibly lets out a slight whimper of humour, but manages to pass it off as a partial tearful outburst.

Even the word gargantuan is bigger than his cock!

Chris seeing her emotional weakening, excuses himself after hugging her one last time, and exits through the door at the end of the office.

Maria sits back in her chair, relieved that her convincing performance has meant that she can now move on to pastures new. Now open to sexual fulfilment she would never have to fake another orgasm. Unable to contain her excitement, she calls Theo and leaves him a message when his answer phone cuts in.

" I've done it T! No more small dicks for me! The only way is up now, I'm on a mission. Let's go out tomorrow night, or the night after. Oh hell, why not both days, I have some serious catching up to do! I'm in need of some serious sexual satisfaction! "

The sound of faint footsteps disappearing from earshot, confuses her slightly. She wonders who it is that is in the top office with her. *It could be Chris. But he wouldn't have stayed around after the inevitable dissolving of their relationship. Perhaps the cleaners are in.* She hears the footsteps dissipating and the sound becoming further and further away.

A few hours later, Maria had finished her proposed development plan for Thornton Heath in Croydon and was taking a much needed break in the canteen. It had been her first real coffee of the day, not the usual vending machine coffees dotted around the office floors, such as the one from the morning. She enjoyed the rich aroma and the frothy sensation of her latte but was soon brought back to reality by the sight of Reuben , her boss, walking towards her.

"Hi Reuben, glorious weather we are having for October, isn't it? I wasn't expecting a clear day *and* a blue sky. " She says artificially.

" Totally agree Maria. " He says smiling awkwardly. " So, what are you doing here today on your day off? "

What am I doing here?! Well, I'm working my ass off so that I can try and get in your good books, and, oh I don't know, maybe fucking impress you for once in my life.

" Just getting on top of things Reuben, the preposition is going really well and I think we have a good chance of securing the development. " She says confidently.

" That's good news." Reuben says avoiding eye contact all the while looking into his Americana. " I have to admit, I'm surprised to see you're here. I expected you to be off spending time with that security guy.. What's his name, Craig ? "

" Its Chris, his name is Chris." She says annoyed at his disdain." We're not together though....well, not anymore."

Reuben locks eyes with hers. "Anymore? " He says intrigued. " Why is that? You seem to act like two love struck teenagers. Wherever he is, there you are, his tongue down your throat, yours down his. To be honest, it's a little bit too much. For the work place that is. When I see you two at it, i feel just as uncomfortable as I did when I walked in on my son ' pleasuring' himself. "

" Well, your won't have to worry about that anymore now sir. " She says frostily.

Reuben looks to to the floor, half sheepishly, half with disapproval. " I'm sorry Maria, that was uncalled for. He looks up into her eyes, coldly. " It really is none of my business who you fuck. "

" Rueben! I'm pretty sure you're being as unprofessional as you can possibly be right now. I'm also definitely not being paid enough to take this shit from you. "

" You're right Maria, my utmost apologies, I think I should go. "

" I agree, I think you should go, before I bring human resources into this. "

" I really didn't mean to cause any offence. If you could get me those figures by twelve on Monday morning that would be most beneficial. I really am sorry Ms Martinez. " He says respectfully as he gets up from his chair and starts to leave.

" Forgiven.. " Maria says coldly as he turns to walk away. She watches him shake his head as he disappears into the lift back to his office.

How fucking dare he judge me that way! ! It's not like I was performing oral sex on Chris in front of everyone during the morning minutes. We didn't exactly flaunt it! Especially since he didn't have anything to flaunt in the first place! Anyway, I'm pretty sure its impossible to fellate a Ken doll.

She nurses her coffee in her hands, the warm comfort of it's strong aromas fill her soul with energy. Energy to suppress what just occurred. Energy to finish the plans that would knock the socks off of her boss.

It was eight at night when Maria was rudely awakened by Chris's hand stroking her hair. At first, the sensation was enjoyable, familiar, almost erotic, but as she regained consciousness those feelings soon changed to uncomfortable.

" Hey, umm, what you doing here? I thought you had gone home." She says removing her head from his reach.

He shows her his watch. " I've been home. Now I'm back. You must have fallen asleep, it's now eight in the evening, it's time for the second part of my shift..."

" Oh shit! I'm supposed to be at Theo's in half an hour. "

He reaches out his hand for hers as she starts to get up.

" Look, Maria, I don't like the way we finished earlier, it's like we didn't say goodbye properly. Do you think I could be inside you again?   Can we make this happen one last time? "

'Oh fuck! I thought I had got out of this! Dammit, I don't know if I have got the energy to pull of a convincing 'When Harry Met Sally.'

Taking her silent response as a sign, Chris leans in behind her, his hot breath condensing on her neck, her body yielding to his touch. She feels the ripples of pleasure flowing up and down her entire body, from her head to her spine. She had to admit, she had never had a problem with his fore-playing skills. He knew her body well enough to make her respond willingly, but he had never seemed to get it as right as he was now. His technique, although formulaic, seemed to carry a new fervour, a new understanding of her body. It was more than electric, it was somehow more immediate, more charged. Just as she was about to think about his mouth moving from her neck to her ear, he was there. His lips brushing ever so lightly from the nape of her neck working his way up to the bottom of her ear lobe, gently alternating from kisses to nibbling. She shudders and almost immediately feels light headed from his touch. She takes a short, shallow breath and holds it in ecstasy as he lifts her onto the desk. With one hand he gently lowers her onto her back, the other, he slips inside her skirt and shapes it around her panties to feel the heat exuding from her body. He rubs her back and forth, the pressure of his hand on her, quick and probing. He watches her arch her back slightly, and moan breathlessly. With his hand still pressed against her, he eases himself onto her and kisses her firm, but tenderly. Maria responds to his advances, her lips lock aggressively with his. She takes a second to realise, this is Chris doing this to her, *this is actually Chris!* She reaches down to where his hand is and feels the warm moistness he has started within her and closes his fingers around her now burning opening.

" Tear them off Chris. " She whispers in his ear. " Don't think about it, just tear them off. "

Chris takes a second to look behind him to check to see if anyone is around, almost as if waiting for approval.

Maria pulls his face back towards her and smiles " It's ok, just do it. "

He rips them effortlessly off her, and replaces his hand back on her body only this time it's her breasts that his attention is focused on. She hears the zip on his trousers, and him removing them and instantly realises what is about to happen, or not, as it always was with Chris. She grabs his hand and removes it from her left breast and guides him back down to where he had been before and guides his fingers back inside her. She moans loudly, biting her lip as he massages her deeply. She can't believe she's actually not having to fake it. His magic fingers circle her G Spot , teasing her as her face contorts in euphoria. *Is it actually possible?? Could he really make me cum for the first time ever?*

Seeing the look on her face and feeling his fingers getting increasingly wet as he strokes and plays with her, he realises how close she is to climaxing. He can feel her becoming more engorged and her muscles clamping around his fingers. His other hand alternates between her breasts, playing with her erect nipples whilst continuing to finger her enthusiastically. Maria's moans of pleasure turn into screams of unrestrained passion as she feels the rise of warmth and the rush of pleasure wash over her whole body as she climaxes uncontrollably, over and over again.

Chris, releases his fingers from her and replaces it with his inadequately sized penis and thrusts inside. Maria, still recovering from her epic experience screams out again, only this time, with lack lustre conviction. She obliges as he grinds inside her ineffectually until he erupts prematurely. He kisses her, laying on top of her.

" Maria, I hope you don't regret what just happened, it just seemed the most fitting way to say goodbye. " He says, nearly out of breath.

She strokes his hair and smiles at him. " Not at all Hun, that was truly amazing, but I must go. Theo is cooking dinner for me, and I'm going to be late. "

" I understand Maria, I need to be heading back to work anyway. " He pulls his trousers up and straightens himself. " I guess I'll see you around at work? Let's not be awkward strangers okay? "

" Of course, no, really, we're good... You were really good in fact. " She says smirking as she walks towards the lift thinking. At *least someone appreciates the overtime I'm putting in."*

CHAPTER 6

" I'm so sorry I'm late Theo. I have no excuse, and I have no reason. I'm just late. " Maria says flushed, as Theo answers the door to his two bedroom, ground floor flat in Rinaldo Road, Balham.

" *Right.* " Theo widens the door, gesturing for her to come in from the cold.

" Okay. so I was getting fingered by my ex. Well, Chris my boyfriend, who's now my ex. You know what I mean, you heard the answer phone message, no? " She says matter of fact.

Theo looks on bemused pointing at the fine sherry in her hand. " I think we might need one of those. Don't you? " He leads her into the living room, the cream coloured walls accentuating the black horse shoe sofa. The oak laminate floor perfectly complementing the six seater dining room table that shares the limelight with the equally impressive fifty two inch television on the far wall. He disappears into the predominantly black gloss finish kitchen and pours them both a glass before shouting to the living room. " So, *just* fingered? "

" Well, he fucked me afterwards, but it didn't count. You know, it's Chris after all. "

Theo snorts " Of course, his dick's like cheesecake, one slice is never going to be big enough to satisfy! "

" Exactly! The bit that made me laugh the most though is when he said, ' You know you want me, I can feel it in you. ' All I could think was, actually I can't, that's the whole reason why we're breaking up in the first place.

Theo nods to himself as he finishes off the Creme fraîche sauce for the Andalusian Chicken. " So, okay, he pleasured you and that's what made you late, but where did the said ' fingering ' take place. Please don't tell me it was another sordid work outing, or I should say ' inning' ? "

" After your abruptness this morning , I don't think you are in any position to judge.... And don't even try to lie to me. I could hear some guy in the background kissing your chest, back, face or I don't know what part of you. So, who is he? " She says tasting the exquisite fortified wine.

" No one, it was the television. There was no man, you just caught me as I was pleasuring myself , simple as. So, back to your office shenanigans, I'm a little confused. If you say you broke up with him today, why were you taking his digits again? " He says surprised by his own quick wit.

Maria leaves the sofa and walks towards the kitchen to join Theo. " Well, I outright lied and told him that his dick was breaking me in two, amazingly and naively, he believed it. He left, I called you. Oh, did I mention what happened earlier? "

" No, but did it involve falling on someone else's dick, by any chance? "

Maria just stares at him without speaking in answer to his comment.

" Sorry, go on. " Theo says returning his attention to the creamy sauce.

Well, as I was saying, there was this whole awkward run in with Reuben. Believe me, If I could have got away with it, I would have given him third degree burns by chucking coffee in his face after the rude way he addressed me over my involvement with Chris. He practically accused me of being the office whore. " She says sitting back down at the dining table in the living room.

" I thought we had discussed this before," He says dishing up the meal and taking a seat next to Maria. " trampy is more fitting than whore. "

" You cant talk, you're a sex addict! I mean, who masturbates at nine in the morning in this day and age? What are you, twelve?!! " She says laughing.

" Well, only I know me and how to get me off, and since Andrew is dead to me now. " He takes a second. " I wish. "

" Wow! What the fuck happened?! Don't get me wrong, I'm glad you've seen the light, but last night you thought the sun shined out of his proverbial ass, what gives? " Maria says putting her knife and fork back onto the plate.

" Not going to happen until we have finished this bottle, and then moved onto the cheap crap I have in the cupboard. " He pauses. " Then finishing with the Grappa. Up until then, he's not worth one single breath from my mouth. He's the mould building up in a wardrobe, he's the shit mark that can't be removed from a toilet pan and he's the cum stain on a two hundred pound mattress. He's just a waste. A waste of ... Everything. " He says taking another glass of Sherry.

" What the fuck did he do? Seriously Theo, I disliked him before, but I really think I need to hate him the way you do right now. "

" Maybe later, I'm not drunk enough yet. " He says reluctantly. " Sooo Reuben? "

Submitting to his unmistakable change of subject she says. " I don't know babe. It's weird, I try so hard to impress him, but all I get is that look.."

" What look? "

"You know, the look of a disappointed father who can't believe his wife has given birth to yet another girl instead of the son he so desperately wanted."

" Maybe he's gay." He says seductively sipping the sherry.

" No T, believe it or not, not everyone in this world is gay. It might feel like it sometimes, but no, he's straight down the middle, but why are you assuming that me being upset with my lack of progression in the company equates to whether Reuben could be attracted to me or not? " She says taking another mouthful of the zesty sauce with the slow cooked chicken.

" Well , it seems to me that you know you're good at your job, and you know the successes that you have within your career. " He formulates.

" And? Your point is? "

" If I have to spell it out then I will. If the above statement is true, which it is, then there must be another reason that you are trying to prove yourself to Reuben. " He looks at her, holding her stare for nearly an uncomfortable amount of time. " Come to think of it, and correct me if I'm wrong, but you won't have to cos I already know I'm right, but when you first started working at the firm, he used to pay you more attention, didn't he? "

She shrugs her shoulder dismissively. " No, I don't think so. "

" No, I'm *sure* he did, you used to come home from work and it was ' Reuben this, and Rueben that. ' "

" Don't be so stupid, I didn't! Where did you get that from? " She trills defiantly.

" No! I'm right, I remember now! One time you even said that he was the first Latino man you've ever found attractive cos I nearly simultaneously choked on an olive and fell off my seat. I was genuinely shocked. "

" Ha ha, very funny! No, you're clearly delusional. It must be someone else you're thinking of. "

" Just admit it Maria! It's not like I'm asking you to shit on my living room floor, I'm just saying you *had* or currently *have* a crush on him. "

" I think I'd rather do that in every room of your flat... after a curry .... and a bottle of white lightening, than admit I like my pig ignorant, tactless boss to be honest with you. " She thinks for a second. " I don't like him, do I? "

" All I'm saying is that, and risking sounding like the biggest cliché ever, there is a very thin line between love and hate. "

Seizing her opportunity to redirect the conversation back to him she interjects. " So, if that's the case, you must love the fuck out of Andrew then. Maybe even bordering on obsession by the sounds of it. "

" I *genuinely* hate him! I'd happily put him in a room full of anger management sufferers wearing a T-shirt saying. ' I fucked all your respective partners last night. ' Rather than let him go anywhere near my ass again. "

" So, *no* Reuben talk, *no* Andrew talk..yet. " She says happily before changing tack. " I seriously need to get myself back out there. I'm not kidding you. With the exception of the ably assisted fingering earlier tonight, I had nearly forgotten how to have an actual orgasm without having to fake it. "

" Well, there's the new barman where I work, he's straight and single. " Maria looks unconvincingly back at him. " I know what you're thinking, that's a new one, but yes, he is totally straight. "

" Thats encouraging! How do you know though Theo? "

Theo sits back in his chair smiling to himself. " Well, after Callum spent the whole night harassing the poor man for pistachio nuts, he just leaned over the bar and said. "Sorry, I know I have impeccable taste and I'm well groomed, but I ain't gay. "

" Callum really is a walking sperm count test isn't he? "

" I know, bless him, I think he's worked his way through the whole city, that now every gay or bi-curious guy in London knows him on a first name basis. "

" Harsh, but completely fair and justified. So, the guy you work with, what's his name, his age and his dick size? And yes, I did just ask that, and I think you'll agree I have a right to ask! I will want answers on my desk by the early part of next week at the latest. "

" His name is Conrad, but everyone calls him Connor and he's thirty two. I don't know the honest answer to the last part for definite, but judging from last week when he got a jug full of woo woo down him after an over zealous hen party member grabbed his ass, the drenching left little to the imagination. Put it this way, I wouldn't have any complaints. "

" Sounds perfect! Finally a real man. " She says optimistically. " So, I'm obviously coming to see you at work.. Maybe we could go to a karaoke bar? "

" Works for me, just promise me one thing. " He says holding her hand and leading her back into the living room. " Don't do your usual Jennifer Lopez song. You know me sis, I have no ethnic diversity, but even I find the reference to Jenny From The Block too obvious a song choice, even for you. "

She glares over at him with sass, but then agrees. " Okay papi you have a point, so you want me to Adele it up? I can bring it. "

His face broadens, his smile spreads.

" Exactly! Bring the pain! Delve deep girl, make me cry, let me feel it, make me understand her weight gain! " He says merrily. The unmistakable sound of a message being retrieved on Skype resonates in both his and her ears. Maria, sensing Theo's uncomfortable shift, leans in eagerly to read the message that has been sent :

' Last night was amazing! Thank you so much sexy, Soooo, do I get to watch you bite your lip in ecstasy again? '

Maria, shocked, stunned, amazed, and open mouthed, turns to Theo and screams. " WHAT THE FUCK HAPPENED LAST NIGHT?! ! "

Knowing he has no excuses left and no delay tactics to use, he takes one more sip from the delicious wine and speaks.

" Fuck! " He says necking the entire glass of wine he was drinking. " Fuck.... Okay, so I'm not going to go into details about last night, *but* I will tell you this much, it was all because I found out last night that Andrew is bisexual. "

" Very funny Theo, and I'm not Latina, I've just been on a sun bed for four hours ! "

Theo, not laughing, stares at her solemnly. " Genuinely, he's as bisexual as you are oversexed. "

"Jesus Christ! I don't know what to say?! I always knew he was a cunt, and I suspected that he would always be capable of cheating, but flicking chick instead of sucking dick... I genuinely did not see that coming! *How, what, where?* Did he at least have the decency to confess it? "

He takes a moment to let the alcohol numb his throat.

" I walked in on him and bumped into her, or more accurately I should say I walked into her breasts. " He refills his glass before continuing. " And believe me, she ain't no naturist friend of his, I could smell the sex all over her, and I'm pretty sure if I hadn't been so flabbergasted I would have *seen* the sex all over her. "

" Jesus Christ! No wonder he was so agreeable to us spending so much time together. I mean I assume this isn't the first time? Did it seem like the first time? "

He looks her dead in the face. " Yes she definitely had that ' I've been fucked on more than one occasion by your gay lover ' look on her face. " He waits for a second before continuing. " Oh, I don't know Maria, believe it or not, it wasn't the first thing that came to my mind! It was more like, THIS PERSON DOESN'T HAVE A DICK! "

" I'm sorry, but I need to hear something encouraging after that shit storm of a story, I need to know some good news, and more importantly, I need to know who this is? " She says turning the laptop towards his face and pointing to the screen. " Who is Kez-zam!? "

He retells the story of last night, everything from the first meeting with Kez in Floridita, to the eventual erotic indiscretion in the partially secluded mini park. She listens enthusiastically as he tells her about his uncontrollable lust and his inability to resist this strong black man who oozed street sophistication all wrapped up in his catwalk model looks. All the while he was talking, the grin that he so desperately tried to suppress, showed itself. With every mention of Kez's firm touch, of every undulating orgasm, of every beautiful word that dropped from his mouth so perfectly into his ears, his voice resonated like a beautiful melody. Yet with every recollection of the joyous events of the previous night, each one was met with a defiant refusal to allow himself to fully appreciate the possibilities of a new love, of a new beginning.

" I would kill for that kind of sexual workout! Are you crazy Theo! What the hell are you doing not replying to him.. *Immediately!* Hell if you don't, I will for you! One of us needs to be getting it regularly! " She says emphatically before her realisation. " Hang on, is there a reason? Is he an ugly tree victim? I need to see a picture of him! "

" I genuinely don't have any pic of him, the only images I have of him are in my head. " He says dreamily.

" And in your ass! " She says finishing his sentence playfully.

She reaches over to him, grabs his face in her warm hands.

" Seriously Theo, just go with it, it's romantic. " He looks at her sarcastically. " So, maybe romantic is pushing it, but it's visceral, animalistic, these are things that shouldn't be overlooked. "

He lays back on the sofa, pulling his legs under himself. " I know what you mean, and don't get me wrong, there were times when I thought I was going to pass out. You know, full on veins popping out of my neck, red faced craziness, but one thing I can't rely on is that base sexuality anymore. It's got me in *so* much trouble before and I'm not about to open myself up to that so soon after Andrew. "

" Well, technically, you already have opened yourself up since Andrew already. " She reaches out her hand to him and grasps it tightly. " Now, I know you expect that I'm going to say something comforting, emotional, and lighthearted. Well, one out of three ain't bad.. Here goes...GET A FUCKING GRIP! This is great sex ! Amazing sex! Perfect sex! Mind blowing sex! Gravity changing sex! IT'S   SEX! Do you understand Theo!? You can't possibly turn this away, can you? "

" I have to admit I haven't stopped thinking about him tonight, in fact all day. I can still smell him on me, I don't think I want to wash for at least a month. " He says lazily stroking the sofa arms.

" Well, you can forget our regular Tuesday night get togethers then if that's going to be your hygiene regime from now on. " She says slyly.

" Okay, enough about him. " He says shaking his head. " Let's get you on a dating site sis. "

" Correction, lets get *US* on a dating website. Since you are clearly not going to take this whole Kez thing seriously, then that means that you are *free* to do this with *me*, right? "

He stifles his hesitation before saying confidently. " Of course, one hundred percent, count me in. I don't want anything serious, so I can just make it clear on my profile. I can see it now, ' Don't fuck with me, just *fuck* me."

She starts to fill in her profile methodically. " So, tomorrow night, eight o clock at Grace? "

Theo shifts along the elegant yet masculine leather sofa and grabs the computer from her. " Hang on, you haven't even chosen a man yet !? "

" Give it here! " She says, snatching it back from him before putting her finger directly on the screen, choosing a random profile without a picture. " This one. "

" *Are you crazy?!* You can't even see a face! It's just blank! He could look like Shrek or worse still, Willem Dafoe! "

" Now, come on Theo! I doubt very much that he has green skin or looks like a real life version of The Joker. " She says taking another gulp of wine. " Besides, he says that he is ' warm, caring and big hearted.... In fact, BIG everywhere. ' according to this. "

" Jesus Christ! In the gay world you'd be called a size queen , you know that? "

" I don't care what I would or would not be called, I just need a big one for once, something that actually makes me feel him, if you catch my drift. "

" Honey, when you talk about cock, it's hardly a drift. It's a fucking blizzard! " He laughs.

" Well, all I know is, is that it's been a very dry year. In fact, no, it's been a total drought, and it's about time it pisses down on me. " She says, concentrating on the screen.

" Point taken, go ahead, send it. "

She hovers over the enter key, and thinks before hesitating. Theo, seeing her hesitation, pushes her finger until it hits the enter key to send the message.

" You're welcome sweetness. " He says cheekily as her pretend outrage melts into an excited smile.

" What now? " She says staring at the screen eagerly.

" Well, nothing in the way you *think* it will. " He stares at her, willing her to figure out what he means. Nothing. " Maria, there's no guarantee he's online at this very second, I'm sure he doesn't have a laptop or mobile device attached to his eyelids. "

" Oh right, I see, my bad. I must seem like such a dating nerd. " She pulls back from the computer before refilling her glass of wine. " So, your turn now T. "

He takes a moment to look through the profiles, each picture leaving him feeling lacklustre. *Too this and too that. I don't get it? Usually I could find someone that sparks my interest by now?*

" Some time tonight would be lovely T! Unless there's something that's stopping you from choosing a random new dark skinned hunk?! Or should I say *someone* that's stopping you? " She cheekily leans in and nudges him lightly on his shoulder.

" Don't be so fucking ridiculous Maria! I've known him less that twenty four hours and you've already got me paired up with him like I'm some hopeful pound dog puppy that stares into the eyes of its new overly excited owner. Next thing you'll be telling me is that you think I'm going to marry him! " His eyes widening even by his own thought process.

She smiles broadly and matter-of-factly. " Of course not.. I mean I'd at least need to see you next to each other to see if you're aesthetically pleasing to the eye.

Another message pings in their ears.

" Looks like someone's keen...." She crosses her legs toward his laptop to read the next message that has popped up on his screen, begging for attention. " Hope you didn't regret last night T, I would be honoured to feel you in my arms again, but this time a movie and dinner first? What do you think? "

Flushed with excitement, he desperately tries to shake the obvious grin materialising across his face. " Give it here." He says under his breath. He types a reply so quickly so as to make sure that Maria can't see what he is writing." There! Done. That's taken care of him, okay so let me get back to choosing the hottest guy I can find for our double date. "

" Are you sure? I mean are you sure you wouldn't just like to invite the oh so sexy Kez instead? Oh, and can you get me some more Sherry? " She says seizing her opportunity to look back at the Skype conversation. She clicks on his name and sees that he does in fact have a profile picture next to his username.

"SOOOOO ! No face picture you say?? Are you sure about that, or is this image of a random catalogue model pic to hide his ugliness? I mean for all I know he could be the dictionary definition of a total arm biter! You could be just painting me this picture because you're so humiliated that Andrew' s infidelity pushed you into the arms of dating roadkill? "

Why didn't I lock the computer? Geez Theo , you should have learnt by now that Maria would have looked. He walks back over to the sofa where Maria's face is glued to the laptop, fake licking the screen. " Yes, that is him, and yes that picture is *exactly* what he looks like, and yes he makes me hard just by looking at his face.. Is that what you wanted to hear Hun? "

She continues to look at him lustfully. " All I can say is that I have become completely aware of my nipples in the last two minutes thanks to the image plastered across the screen. Why are you gay men so handsome? Is it really that much to for me to ask for a guy that doesn't look like he's inbred? Or worse still, a football supporter? " She continues to stare at his picture from all angles. " Does he have a single brother, cousin, or even a hot uncle. Hell I'll even settle for a silver fox grandad? "

" Let me think... Now come to mention it, he did say that he had a good looking older brother as his dick made it's way up into my asshole. Also, I think he mentioned his cousin was available as he shoved me up against the wall and stuck his tongue in my ear.. Of course I don't know! " He says sarcastically.

" Ha ha! Well, next time, maybe you could try being a little less selfish and think about me when his cock is firmly placed in your chocolate whizz way . I'm not asking much when you think about it really! "

" I'll do my best to keep that in *my head* when I'm next giving *him head.* " He thinks quickly. " although there won't be a next time since he and I were just a one night stand.... Can we move this along? I mean I'm more excited about what we will be eating tomorrow? "

As Maria was about to reply with the entire menu memorised from their many visits, unexpectedly a message appears on the screen. Assuming it would be Kez, Maria hoards the computer to see the next salacious message only to see that it is for her.

" Oh my! Looks like I have a date already! And I didn't even have to put a picture up myself! I must be good! " She says excitedly.

" Wow, he's keen. " Theo leans in to read the message out loud. " Hi there, I hope you don't think I'm being too forward, but I'm a firm believer in getting to know someone in reality as opposed to hiding behind words on a screen. When you free for a drink? " He looks over at Maria before typing. " Tomorrow would be perfect, seven o clock good for you? "

The message beeps eagerly again.

" Excellent! He's free! " She claps her hands together.

" So hot stuff, you *still* haven't chosen one, and since you don't even want a serious boyfriend you only have to chose a random person. Just pick one, it can be anyone. "

He thinks about it for a minute. " Now you put it like that, I might as well go on a date with Steven the guy who's been hounding me for years now, he wouldn't take no for an answer even when he knew I was with Andrew. " He takes his phone out and starts typing a message and within minutes he's got the confirmation he knew he would.

" So, where were we? "

" I *think* you were about to pour me another glass of wine? "

CHAPTER 7

Maria leans in to kiss the handsome stranger after spending the best part of five hours listening to every intelligent, interesting, and funny thing that fell from his beautiful mouth. He leans in across the table, accepting her lips passionately. Gentle at first, then with more commitment, he lets his tongue caress the top of her mouth. The deserted restaurant seems to hold it's breath in anticipation of their next move, their next progression. The stranger gently puts his hand under the table until he reaches his desire. Her warmth. He feels the moisture flow from her, and the heat increase as she gasps and swallows his tongue powerlessly. They kiss passionately blissfully unaware that Ne Yo has appeared in the room and is treating their ears to his smooth vocals. The sound of birds chirping merrily fill the air with their own sweet song.. In an instant, she wakes from her dream.
" Why now?! " She groans. " It seems like the sex dreams are lasting just as long as the real thing lately! "

She looks at the time, closes her eyes and attempts the near impossible task of reconnecting with the handsome stranger in her dreams for a few more minutes. She thinks about the possibilities of the up and coming blind date. The exciting adventure of a new man and more importantly for her, a man who hopefully knows his way around a woman. In contrast, she recalls the events of last night with Chris and the relief she had felt that he had accepted the termination of their relationship so readily. She thinks about how easy it had been, and why she hadn't done it sooner instead of putting up with the undeniable incompatibility between them. *Why do we let things go on when they're clearly not working? Why are we, as a nation, so willing to settle for second best? Why do we fall in to uncomfortable comfortableness ?* She emerges from the covers and crawls out of bed and makes her way to the kitchen. The bright sunshine flooding through the bamboo shutter blinds seem to further illuminate her current thoughts.

She makes herself a coffee and savours the dawn of a rare, clear day on a majority gloomy October. Her phone, still on silent, lights up next to her. It's Amelia. " Hey sis, how did it go? I was thinking about you after I left for work. " She yawns as she reaches for a croissant from the bread bin.

" It was okay. Actually, it was surprisingly good. I mean obviously we had an almighty row that rivalled anything you've ever heard or seen on a Friday night in Croydon."

" Don't you mean *any* night in Croydon? " Maria chirps in.

" I'm just going to have to be patient with him until he feels he can trust me again. If of course he can.. But for now, it's okay. " Amelia answers, quite cheerfully.

" Well, I'm happy for you, I think." She says checking the clock on the small widescreen television on the wall to make sure she has time to make it in to work for another busy day. " So, how did he feel about you telling him he's so big for you? I'd imagine a big part of him liked that, because what man is going to hate hearing that his appendage is huge. That's like saying he's too rich, or too good looking, or he's got too much food on his plate to contend with. "

Amelia giggles. " Believe me, that was the one saving grace, and it's the thing that's making it easier for him to deal with. He seems to think that he and I can work through this. Although how he plans to shorten his dick, or hollow me out without surgery, I don't honestly know. " She pauses before changing the subject. " Listen though Maria, I really do want to say thanks again, I don't think I could have got through it without you, it was a big deal. "

" Of course you could sis, you've had to deal with big things before... *Big things* coming out of you and big things going in you. You're stronger than you think you are, *you know?* " She hears her sister sigh. " Okay, I really have to get going now, if I don't then my boss will .. will.. will continue to under appreciate me and more than likely not even realise I've turned up late. "

" What it is to be wanted and needed eh? Right, well I have an important date I have to keep with Peppa Pig , so you're not the only one who has to be around a swine for hours upon hours every day. See you later Hun. "

She takes her coffee to the bathroom and continues with her morning routine. Stepping into the shower she allows herself, once again, to be distracted by the man in her dreams. She hadn't realised how exciting it would feel to know that there is a man out there this morning, hopefully thinking of her too with the same anticipation. With the same optimism. She thinks about all the pros and cons of the night to come as she finishes cleaning and moisturising, hastily finishes her coffee and rushes off to the bus stop outside her flat.

As she walks through the revolving doors at the entrance to work, she can't help but feel a shift in atmosphere. It seems palpable, almost physical. She elegantly glides across the Aztec style marble floor to catch the elevator to her office floor, flashing her usual confident seductive smile to the receptionist and security guards, yet something didn't feel right. They seem to be avoiding her eye contact.

" Don't be crazy! " She says out loud, fidgeting uncomfortably as the empty lift starts. *Why would you think this? You have done nothing wrong.* The lift opens on the first floor and Chris's best friend and work colleague, Martin, walks in. He takes one look at her, shakes his head, steps inside, and faces away from her, sneering to himself.

" Okay, what was that? " She says demanding an answer.

" What was what? " He says, still looking straight forward.

" That ! " She says shaking her head in exaggeration.

He looks back at her. " I'm not pointing the *finger* at anyone. No one is to blame. "

She takes a sharp breath. " *Did Chris tell you what happened?!?!* "

" Don't worry, I get it. My man Chris, he wasn't always as *hands* on as he could have been. " He says, this time clearly amused by his own comments.

Realising what his friend was saying behind his double entendres, she raises her voice." *That motherfucker, I can't believe he told you!!* "

" Told me what Maria? I really have no idea what you're talking about. "

" Don't even start to pretend you didn't just say *finger* and *hands*, he *told* you...*BASTARD* ! ! " She snarls as she stamps her foot in anger.

 At that moment, the doors to the lift opens and he walks out, but before the doors close again he looks back at her. " Oh, and Maria, for the record, he *didn't* tell me, I could *see* it all for myself. "

Angered by his attitude and puzzled by the riddle of his parting sentence, Maria attempts to calm herself down. *Okay, so he knows*. She breathes calmly and checks her mirror to make sure the redness in her face is slowly leaving her. *I guess I couldn't expect anything else from Martin, since that was his best friend... But what did he mean, I could see it for myself? I mean, who does he think he is, fucking Yoda? I don't believe that he is that perceptive or sensitive for one minute, out of the two of them, he made Chris look like a new age man!* She focuses her attention back to the ascending lights on the buttons of the lift and prepares to walk out on to her floor.

The doors open and the sound of the buzz of the floor is the serenity she needs to get herself back on track.

" Morning Sandy... How are you Jerome? " She says flashing her newly restored winner smile.

Nothing. No answer, not even a preoccupied acknowledgment. Within seconds she was back to the person she thought she had left behind in the lift.

Don't panic Maria, just get to your office and get started. You need to get a grip. It's eight o clock in the morning, I know gossip can travel fast, but there's barely been time for everyone to have even taken their morning coffee.

She was just about to walk through the door to the aforementioned safe haven when she hears someone across the room whispering and giggling. She tunes in to the fragmented sentences. She hears ' nasty ' and ' exhibitionist ' and then finally she catches one full sentence.. " Check your emails, twelve minutes past one in the morning, it's unbelievable! "

Maria closes the door quietly, trying to draw as little attention to herself as possible. She sits down in her chair and boots up her computer. She looks outside at her work colleagues and all she can see is a sea of sniggering, disgusted and awkward faces.

" *Come on you stupid email!* " She says frantically typing her password incorrectly numerous times in her panic to log on. "*What the hell have you done Chris, what have you done??* " The anticipation nearly killing her, she opens her emails. There in front of her screen, the timed email of twelve mins past one.

' Subject Matter. Farewell Maria & Chris. '

No actual writing, just an email containing an mpeg. Feeling the dread clambering up her entire body, she clicks on the video and the true horror of what he has done is revealed.

There, in front of her like an outer body experience, was her laying out on the office table from the night before. The image clearly showing Chris pleasuring her with his fingers.

Maria reels back in her chair and let's out an almost silent scream. She covers her hand across her mouth as a mixture of tears and sweat cover her face. *This is really happening, he has really done this!!* She slowly watches the video, unable to move. Transfixed. She closes the video down. " I think I'm going to be sick." She reaches for one of the barley sugars on her desk to try and calm her, now turning stomach, and throws one in her mouth. *How could he do this? He must have known it would be the end of us both at the company?! The selfish bastard! The childish, selfish, evil bastard!!*

She looks up at the glass wall facing out into the office. The play school antics and hurtful taunts of her co workers were now replaced by a busy office ticking away like clockwork. Before she could even take a second to figure out why everything had changed, the door to her office flings open to reveal a bitterly disappointed looking Rueben.

" My office Maria.. Now please.. " He says solemnly.

Maria, unable to even speak, stands up and follows him swiftly to his office. She walks in and waits for him to ask her to sit.

" Maria, I don't think I need to explain why we are having this conversation, but at the same time I am forced to acknowledge that what has taken place is without a shadow of a doubt, gross misconduct. " He says quietly.

Maria, still standing, starts to feel herself wobble and shake. *This can't be happening, it really has to be a dream, fucking hell Maria wake the fuck up! I don't want to do this anymore!* Without warning, her eyes haze over and she slumps to the floor.

A few minutes pass and Maria awakens in a comfortable reclining chair with a very different, concerned Reuben staring back at her.

" Are you okay Maria? I can tell this has come as quite a shock to you. I assume it is safe to say, that you had no idea he was going to do this? " He says, sat resting on the end of the glass table.

She looks at him squarely. " No I knew, couldn't you tell? *Didn't you see the way I winked at the camera with that knowing look* ? "

" Sorry? " He says confused.

Unable to believe that he hasn't picked up on her sarcasm she continues. " Yes, if you look really carefully you'll see me mouthing, did you not see it ? I'm saying " How's my tits look from this angle???? "

Finally understanding what she means, Reuben interrupts.

" Maria.. I "

" Oh and in case you're wondering. This.. " She points to herself in her entirety. " Me falling down like a sack of shit, that's just me too. I often have spontaneous moments like this, I'm just thankful I didn't wake up in a puddle of my own piss and shit! *Of course I didn't know Rueben!* If I *knew*, do you honestly think I would have done it in the first place??! "

" I'm just so disappointed in you Maria, and it saddens me so much that I have no choice but to suspend you and Chris until further notice. I suggest you and Chris take some time to think about the consequences of what has happened. If, going forward, the decision is made to keep you both on, you will need to seriously question whether you should, or could maintain a relationship that is professional in the workplace. "

" Well, I'll be sure to make sure I tell him that when we are eating dinner and drinking wine tonight in our cosy little existence. "

He looks on perplexed again.

" Oh for Christ's sake Rueben! We aren't together anymore! I told you that yesterday in the canteen !! That's the whole reason we did what we did! It was break up sex! Stupid, public break up sex, but never the less, it was break up sex... It's over! "

His face, for the first time since she had walked through the door into his office, lightened. Some of the weight, laying above his eyes alleviated.

" I think it's best Maria. " He reverts back to his concerned face before speaking again.

" You will be paid for the full two weeks suspension and we will be in touch with the   decision of the outcome. I'm really sorry. If there was anything else I could do, I would, but it's out of my hands. "

He leans in, takes her hands a little too familiarly, and squeezes them in comfort. There is a knock at the door. It's Martin from earlier waiting outside to escort her off the premises.

" Seriously Reuben! You have known me for years, do I *really* need to be escorted out? What do you think I'm going to take? She looks over at the still smirking security man. " Oh, and if I *have* to be shown out, it is DEFINITELY not going to be him! "

Rueben gestures to the man to leave.

" Of course Miss Martinez, then I will walk you out myself. " He says sympathetically.

Five minutes of walking, and watching as her colleagues quietly nod their heads towards her, they arrive at the entrance to the building. As she starts to walk, he follows until he too, is standing outside, next to her.

" Now that I'm technically away from the company, I need to say something to you Maria. " He looks awkward in his stance.

" What Reuben? Is this the part where you tell me that you always hated me, that I was never good enough at my job for you??!! " She says bitterly as the tears start to well again.

He looks at her, genuinely shocked.

" Quite the opposite actually, I just wanted you to know, whatever the outcome, I thank you for being a dedicated hard worker, a great team player, and you always worked to the highest levels of your ability.

Not forgetting that you did all of this with utmost professionalism at all times... "

She looks back at him and smiles weakly. " Thank you Reuben, but I think we can *both* agree I'm *not* professional at all times or else I wouldn't be out here on the streets as I am right now. "

He smiles back at her with a warm handshake. " I know you may think I've been a right royal pain in the backside, but I hope you know, it wasn't anything.... Well, you know. "

" Well, actually I don't know."   Sensing his awkwardness she brushes over his bumbling before adding, " And maybe I'm not supposed to know either. Take care Rueben, and I'll wait for the boards decision. "

She turns and walks back into the street, glancing back a few times to see when Reuben re-enters the building. Finally, after a good two minutes she reaches for her phone and calls Theo.

" Maria?! Is that you? " He says, struggling to make out one word through her sorrow. " I ain't no dog whisperer, so if that's you, please answer me Hun. That voice is kind of freaking me out a little. I feel like I'm going to look behind me and some madman will be there ready to gut me with an axe! "

" *I've lost my job!* " She eventually vocalises through the tears." Chris set me up! He recorded everything on the surveillance video and then sent it as an attachment to everyone in the office. I feel so humiliated... and then Rueben came in, and well, you can guess the rest. "

" Oh Maria! I don't know what to say! Have you been fired or suspended? "

" Suspended, but we both know that I don't stand a chance of keeping my job. " She suddenly remembers their date night is tonight. " Honey, there is no way I can go on a date tonight. I can't take the chance of having two failures in one day. I'd be hanging myself from the restaurant chandelier after one glass of rosé. "

" I agree, point taken, in that case I'm taking you out tonight and we are going to get completely smashed. I'm talking, *so gone* that we were never even here. " He hears the hesitation in her voice. " Oh and I forgot to mention, it's all on me. I've had a very good month with tips and also I got paid from the gig I did at O' Reilly's, so you have to say yes. "

" Yes Theo, I'd love that, in fact I *need* that.. I want to even forget my own name tonight. "

" Of course, we will get you so drunk you'll be that numb that you won't know if it's the alcohol you're drinking or if you're having a stroke! " He says wickedly. " OH! I've just had an idea, my work mates have booked a private karaoke party at Maison Touareg tonight, I'm certain they won't care if we add two more people to the list. We are going to kill it on stage. "

" Well, if we are drinking as much as I expect we will, then we will be murdering it, more like." She says brightening a little.

" So, eight o clock sound good for you Hun? " He asks.

" Let me see I finish work at... Oh, hang on, that's right, I don't have a job now. So I will be busy drinking the cheapest wine I can find on offer at Tesco until you're ready to go. "

" Great! That's my girl, okay, so scrap meeting at the bar, I'll finish the laundry and then I'll be over to help you drink that wine. It's a tough job, but someone has to do it. "

" Thank you Theo " She says , audibly more herself. " Thank you. "

Three bottles of the cheapest red wine, and one bottle of value vodka later at Maria's, they head towards the Moroccan and Lebanese restaurant on Greek Street to sing their hearts out in protest of the men who have wronged them for the past few years.

" Right! I'm going to get us in the mood with a rendition of Joss Stone - You Had Me, You Lost Me, first. Then I'll somehow end with Stevie Wonder - For Once In My Life, just so that we don't come across as two jaded hacks who hate men with every bone in our bodies. "

" Well, I personally don't care if I come across as man hating. In fact I don't even care if the hatred that seeps through every word I'm singing on that stage makes me come across as some man hating, militant lesbian ! " She says tipsily.

A couple of women leaving the restaurant's riad style doorway, look distastefully at Maria after her outburst.

" Ummm might need to reign it in a bit sis, I don't really want to get chucked out before we have even entered the place. " Theo says smiling apologetically to the women, who accept reluctantly.

As they step through the door, the unmistakeable smell of Ras El Hanout warms the air with it's notes of lavender, rose petals and cassia, ending in a cayenne and cinnamon kick. The contrast of the bright lights of the city outside, to the warm, low level lighting, ruby red walls intertwined with Arabic artwork transports them to holiday memories in Morocco years ago. They look around at the myriad of tea candles encased in red tipped holders and the low hanging atlas lanterns and it is only then they are hit by an instantly recognisable voice. One that is neither amazing, nor awful, yet full of confidence and attitude...unmistakably Callum.

" Hey guys! What he fuck are you doing here on a week day?! " He says halfway through his performance, causing the rest of the group to laugh raucously and turn towards Maria and Theo.

Theo smiles and blows him a kiss across the room and puts his hand up. Seeing this, a man who has had his eye on Callum during the whole performance, attempts to join him on stage.

" Honey, you think you can afford this?! " He says playfully.   " Trust me, I spend more on cologne in one week than you do on your entire months shopping, so move along child! "

Laughing at Callum' s outrageous public display, Maria and Theo walk to the intimately sized bar and take a seat on the statuesque wooden chairs and order a couple of glasses of Muscatel de Ksara.

" Here's to being single, not wanting to mingle, would rather stay home and eat a Pringle, cos I can make my own self

 tingle. " Theo says toasting Maria as they drink a large gulp of the sweet wine. He leaves the drink in Maria's capable hands as he walks towards the karaoke host and requests his song before returning to her.

" So, what's next for you love? " He shouts, competing with the finale to Callum' s song.

" Do you know what ? I really don't have a clue T. " She states with a semi smile. " What do you think? What can you see me doing? "

" A sex therapist, or working in a sex shop, ooh! Maybe a sex toy tester? " He grins.

" Ha ha, very funny! Well at least I don't run away from great sex like it's the school bully, Mr ' I've-had-some-of-the-best-sex-in-my-life-but-I-don't-want-to-pursue-it-cos-I'm-more-of-a-pussy-than-Garfield.' "

" Well, I *was* going to say you are *way* better than that job anyway and that now you can find something that will make you truly shine, but now I'm just sticking with the original statement. Oh, or a high class hooker? What do you think? "

Not knowing Maria and Theo's humour, a couple of people surrounding them look stunned at their comments to each other. They smile at each other and continue to rib.

" Up next.. Theo! Can you come to the stage please Theo? " A overly muffled voice booms through the restaurant.

The room claps encouragingly as he takes to the front and the music blares out. Theo's soulful, emotive vocals fill the room and the candles become his floating lighters in the air.

The crowd, previously disengaged with Calum's vocal performance, seem captivated by his authentic rendition of the Joss Stone classic.

Theo, smiling from ear to ear, scans the room making sure to include everyone in his performance. He looks out through the glass window of the restaurant and notices a familiar silhouette staring back at him. As he focuses, he realises that it's Kez. The man who had taken him to sexual ecstasy, and had held him all night long so tenderly after his painful discovery, was now attempting to enter the restaurant. Seeing that it was a private party, Theo visually signals to let him in. Theo determined to not lose his concentration amidst the excitement of seeing him standing metres away from him, smiles knowingly at him. Kez, now mesmerised by Theo's vocal talent, smiles intensely and winks back at him. Unable to stop himself from staring, he mouths the word ' Wow! ' and waits excitedly to see Theo.

Theo continues to work the room, using the full range of his falsetto, executing one run after another. He momentarily looks over at the object of his desire only to see that Callum has made his way over to him. Bemused and slightly confused, Theo looks on as Callum appears to be trying to talk to Kez.

It looks like more than talking... No! This is hysterical! He's flirting with him! Why though? He moves over to the right to take a closer look, and it's then that he realises.*Callum doesn't recollect that he has met him last night and was rejected publicly and, by the looks of it, is about to be again. 'Wow! Callum really is a whore, he doesn't even remember who he's made a move on a day ago!* He let's out a slight laugh but quickly remembers that he's still in the middle of the song.

A minute later, followed by rapturous applause, Theo hurriedly walks over to Kez.

" Baby! You are seriously gifted, and I'm not even talking about how well you suck dick! " He shouts above the applause. " Theo, you need to be mine, I crave you! I haven't been able to stop thinking about you all day. " He grabs his waist and kisses him hungrily. " *Trust me*, I'm not used to feeling this much for someone I just met less than a day ago! " He looks into his eyes. " *You're amazing!* "

" Thank you so much, that is so nice of you.. " He says smiling, sweat still glistening on his forehead from his performance. Kez takes his silk napkin and mops him tenderly. " So, can I see you again soon? "

Theo looks over at Maria. She waves over in his direction, spilling her drink as she motions him to rejoin her at the bar as countless men circle her. " Soon, I promise, but I have to go and look after my best friend now because as you can see, shes getting all that unwelcome attention. Plus, I'm pretty sure she doesn't want to add rape to the supremely shitty day she's having right now. She lost her job today and I'm trying to make sure she forgets her crap even if it is for just a few hours, you understand? "

Kez, looks deflated, but sees the sincerity in his eyes. He takes Theo's face in his hands and kisses him softly. " Of course my little white Wonder. Call me when you.."

Theo, feeling arms wrap around his back turns to see it's Callum. " Amazing as ever boo! You killed it, and not like ' a fart in a library ' way. You killed it in a stylish, sexy way, like Sharon stone in Basic Instinct." He sees the unamused look on Kez's face and turns to Theo. " Oops my bad, talking of farts, bad smells etc, I'd better get myself off.." He says eyeing up his next unsuspecting victim across the room, and continues. "

..so that I can *get myself off* . Before I go though, don't forget the audition tomorrow at the Excel centre, nine o clock, don't be late. It took me ages to get you on the list. Now, just be aware that there will be loads of people there tomorrow who have been on a waiting list for months though, so *please* don't let on that you've only known about it for five minutes. "

" What the fuck Callum! You never told me the date of it last time we spoke! "

" Chill T! What difference does it matter? Now you know, no big deal. " He says, oblivious to Theo's reasoning.

" *The big deal,* " he says, hands framing his forehead and temples, " is that I wouldn't be drinking right now if I was singing tomorrow. Do you understand? Plus, I certainly wouldn't be staying out this late either! "

" Oh! Now I get it. My bad. Sorry! " He looks back in the direction of the guy he was eyeing up before and gestures towards him leaving. " Sorry again..Got to go hun! Catch you later! Love you baby! "

Kez looks at Theo. " I really don't *get* him. By all means, help me to understand, but I don't see what is so great about *him* ? " He says reattaching his arms around Theo's waist.

Their embrace is abruptly interrupted by yet another person, this time the drunken arms of Maria wrap themselves around Theo making Kez release his arms from Theo.

" Oh my god! You *are* real!? " She slurs, as she looks Kez up and down. She looks back at Theo and says. " You did *really well*, and I mean *REALLY* well for yourself T! I'm Soooo happy I finally get to meet you! " She screams, releasing her grip on Theo and shakes his hand instead. " Kez, isn't it? "

He smiles and laughs warmly with her. " Yes it is, and it's lovely to meet you too. Maria? Isn't it? "

" Guilty. " She says reluctantly letting go of his warm, strong hand. " Glad to see he considers me a good enough friend to remember to mention me in between all the fucking I'm sure you guys have been doing. "

" Maria! " Theo says through gritted teeth.

" Oh please! Don't act like you're just sitting in the living room drinking tea and watching East Enders. So, let's not waste any more time, let's get you a drink! In fact let's all get drinks. I'm nowhere near as drunk as I should, or need to be. "

" I'm sorry Maria, but we have to go. Callum neglected to tell me the audition is tomorrow! "

" Typical Callum, you got to love him though, but equally you got to shake the hell out of him for being so inconsiderate. In the end though, it's impossible to stay mad at him. " She says mentally undressing Kez. Her thoughts cut short by her phone vibrating in her jacket. " Back in a minute Hun. You guys are okay right? "

Theo looks over at Kez as if to indicate to him from his previous question that that is the reason why Calum is worth it.

Theo and Kez continue to talk as they wait for Maria to rejoin them. They listen to the barrage of bad singers who continue to humiliate themselves on stage before heading straight to the bar for their complimentary free drink for entertaining the room.

" Is your friend okay? She's been gone a while. "

Theo looks at his watch. " I guess she might have gone to the loo, and you know the queues for the ladies toilets are always longer than the ones generated from Jurassic Park. "

The noise of another phone, this time Theo's, chimes in his pocket. Kez leans in and slowly pulls it out of his back pocket, seizing the opportunity to grab his ass firmly as he hands it over to him. Theo smiles broadly at Kez's hands cupping his rear as he looks at the text message. It's Maria.

" I can't believe it! She's gone home with Leon! I should have seen this coming.."

" Who's Leon babe? " He says still holding his bottom firmly.

" An old ex of hers, and I know the only reason she's gone back with him.. "

" Too obvious to say sex? " Kez says smiling, knowingly.

Theo nods. " Sex, yes.. but sex with a massive dick. "

" Shes an adult though, she can handle herself though, no? "

" *She* can definitely handle herself, but I'm more worried about him. "

" Ah, come on Theo, he will be fine. He is probably just horny, and you know what they say, " better the devil you know. "

Theo, biting his lip, looks anxious.

" What's wrong baby, you can tell me.. I want to help. " Kez says looking deeply into his eyes.

" The thing is when they used to date, he did not take it well when they were done. It took him months and months for him to get over her and... it. "

" It? "

" Maria was pregnant.. but she miscarried. "

CHAPTER 8

" Don't tell me, I can already guess! It probably goes something like this. " Theo starts to mimic Maria's voice and actions as he makes his way through the crowds of people on the way to his audition at the Excel Centre. " *What was I thinking? Why didn't you stop me! If only I hadn't drunk that much last night, it's your fault Theo!* "

She goes quiet. " Okay, have you finished? "

He looks on at a group of people in front of him laughing at his skit. " You know me Hun, I could go on for days, but go ahead. Continue. "

" I was actually going to say that from today, I'm looking into becoming a nun or one of those cat ladies cos I'm pretty sure they don't have sex either.. Seriously! I can't believe I did what I did last night!! It wasn't even a mistake, it was a mistake of epic proportions! "

" *I know*, ex boyfriends are ex boyfriends for a reason Hun. Did he mention, well, you know what? "

" He did, after the sex. Which by the way, was just as amazing as before. So on a selfish note, I finally remembered what it feels like to be sore from a workout that's not down to a treadmill. "

Theo laughs uncontrollably, oblivious to the fact that he has finally arrived at the bottom of the steps leading up to the pyramid of glass that leads to the entrance. " Amen to that sister. So, what exactly did he say? How was it left? Come on, I haven't got that long before I have to start lining up in the queue and pretending that I don't know how good I am. "

" What?? No! Did you just say what I think you said? " She says laughing out loud.

" Oh my! I didn't realise I was capable of that level of arrogance.. I actually feel a little disgusting now. "

" Disgusting *now*, or filthy *last night* ? "

" Well, I have news for you. We didn't do anything if you must know. "

" Not buying it ! You've got more chance of making me think you're a pre operative transsexual, than believing that pile of shit! "

" Honestly! I kid you not! Hard as it may seem. We took a taxi back to mine, and I was just getting myself out, ready to pretend that we should ' call it a night ' before getting ragged senseless up against the bathroom shower wall.. "

" See, I knew I was right. " She says triumphantly.

" No! You're wrong! He just kissed me, said his good nights, and got back in the taxi. Gone. "

" Ooh! That's an anti climax.. Perhaps it was for the best. What do you think? "

" I'm not really sure, it might have been in light of me having to get up early to go to this audition. If that's the case, then I totally understand. Or, it could be that he might have thought I was making excuses because of the whole cunt chops thing. "

" I'm assuming that's Andrews new name? " Her smile evident in her voice.

" Bingo! " He strongly confirms. " Either way, it's not a problem, you and I are still going on that date. Besides, as I mentioned before, I'm not about ready to get my heart broken anytime soon. "

" Not for a couple of weeks at least. " She says cheerily.

" Touché, " He responds as he turns back around, the epic size of the Excel Centre now in full view. " Look, I have to get myself registered and all that bullshit, but before I go, you didn't say.. "

" Oh, right, I forgot that I didn't. " She says unconvincingly.

" Well, we were laying in bed, limbs intertwined, cuddling before sleep and all of a sudden he says. " Was it my fault? "

" What? "

" That was my response. *Exactly.* "

" Why on earth would he think it was anybody's fault? Sometimes sad things happen," he says genuinely. " and most of the times in life, we have no control over them happening in the first place. "

" Of course ! So, I asked him to explain what he meant. He thinks it's his fault because the night before the morning I lost the baby, we had quite vigorous sex. He thinks he somehow dislodged our baby! "

" Bless him, he never was that switched on. I feel awful that he must have been carrying that around for all this time. "

" You feel awful! Imagine how I felt when he said that! " She tears up a little bit. " It gets worse though, the stupid part of it is that getting caught up in all the emotion of the Chris thing, the job and the afterglow of sex and the memory of our baby..."

" Oh no, why do I feel like I want to hang up the phone before you make a revelation worse than when you told me you eat spam straight out of a can? "

" ..when he asked me if we could try to be lovers again, I said yes. "

" Damn it! Maria, shit! " He stops for a second to think. " Unless it's what you actually want? "

" Obviously I'm still attracted to him. Physically at least. Oh and risking sounding superficial, let me tell you this, somebody's been to the gym since we stopped dating! "

" More bumps and lumps than a school canteen rice pudding? "

" So much so, that I questioned if he had had an allergic reaction to something he'd eaten. He was that pumped up. "

" Very nice, it's the same with Kez, I don't think I've ever been with a guy with such a strong powerful body. He literally makes me feel so safe in his arms.

Anyway, back to you. So physically he's off the chart..
What else? I'm trying to remember before everything
happened, were there any issues other than *that*? "

" No real issues, but I worry that eventually those
feelings of loss might dominate our interaction.
Probably not at first, but as time goes by it will
become the old chestnut of the elephant in the room.
"

" I understand, and it won't just sit there either, it will
be nudging you with it's trunk, shitting on the floor,
and just generally breaking everything it touches. "
He says slowly climbing the steps.

" Not to mention the smell either, you'd never get that
out of the carpet. It would be a massive *tusk*. " She
giggles.

" I'll pretend I didn't hear that awful joke and I'll put
it down to you being overtired from all the sex you
had last night. "

" I'd appreciate it if you did. So, before I let you go,
we're still on for tomorrow night? Date night, right?
You did get a reply didn't you? "

" Definitely. "

" Quickly, what's his name. " She demands.

" Stephen, I told you already. " He says swiftly, " See,
you didn't think I was telling the truth, did you?
Andrew really hated him texting all the time. Did I
mention though that he is gorgeous too! "

She tuts before saying sarcastically. " Oh how
surprising, because the guys you normally date are

such ugly dogs. I often feel so bad for the slim pickings that you are left with when I get all the hunks. "

" Bitter much? "

" As lemons. " She says cheekily.

A voice over a loud speaker requesting the applicants to come to one of the registering desks, jolts Theo. " Right, got to go, wish me luck. "

" I'll be hoping that you don't suck. "

" Cute, very cute. Have you been saving that one up."

" Maybe. Seriously though Theo, just kill it the same way that you did last night and they will be begging for you to be on their label. Call me later and let me know how it goes. "

" Thanks sweetness, laters. "

Theo approaches the desk and introduces himself to the overtly friendly assistant. After a few minutes of taking his details and the obligatory personal questions, he is given a map with the directions.

He walks for what feels like a mile through the centre. On the left, he can see seminars being taken and a number of functions in every other room on the right. Eventually he reaches the large glass doors at the end of the building which leads out onto a multi layered set of steps leading to a huge queue. As expected it spanned across the full length and width of the grounds with thousands of hopefuls doing scales and drinking bottles of water to stay hydrated for the long day ahead.

He makes his way to the back of the queue, and prepares for the excessively long wait to be auditioned. *If ever there was a time when I have plenty to think about, this was definitely it. Can I seriously allow myself to open myself up to this new man so soon after the rawness and betrayal Andrew has brought to my doorstep? I know he isn't the same man as him, far from it , but I can't help but tell myself logically, be careful.* This thought angers him more because up until Andrew, he refused to see the negative in anyone. More importantly, he made it a point to not judge another from the experiences he has had in the past. Yet here he was, doing exactly that. Here is this incredibly genuine, unbelievably romantic, beautiful man who unashamedly wants him and all he can think about is the day he's going to be let down by him. The phone rings and without thinking about it, he answers without seeing who it is.

" Thank goodness you picked up, please don't hang up! " The desperate voice of Andrew fills Theo's ears.

" Oh fuck it's you! Why are you wasting your rancid breath on calling me? Go and die of some venereal disease in some sad ass whore house! Just in case you are in any doubt at all. I hate you with every fibre of my body! Just saying your name, makes me feel like I'm going to throw up every meal I've eaten since being breast fed!! That's the extent of how repugnant

I find you!! " He takes a breath, blissfully unaware of how his animated rantings have attracted the attention of the entire crowd.

" Come on Theo, you don't know the whole story. For all you know, it was just a friend. You're too quick to judge me! "

Theo laughs incessantly at the ridiculous statement.

" I'm sorry, but if you honestly expect me to believe that the naked woman stood in front of me, emerging from *your* bedroom as you, *also* naked in bed, watch on, half mast, is *your FRIEND* !? You must be crazier than I thought. Do you *actually think I was born yesterday?! Go FUCK YOURSELF!* There is more chance of me getting struck by lightening, whilst being run over by a car, as I juggle fire balls and memorise every stop on the London Underground than you EVER seeing me naked again!!! "

The whole crowd erupts with applause in support of Theo, as, simultaneously the loud speaker bursts into life again.

" Congratulations from The Excel Centre for being selected for the auditions! "

The phone goes silent and a few seconds later a text comes through informing Theo that he is coming to see him.

" Bollocks, he must have heard the announcement! " He blurts out.

His mind races for a second as he thinks about leaving his space in the queue to escape, to go anywhere. Anywhere that Andrew can't corner him helplessly. Frustrated at the situation he continues to dissect the predicament, weighing up the pros and the cons.

A group of girls in front of him turn and face him. " I hope I'm not overstepping the mark, but we're here for you sweet . If that asshole does turn up, we will make it unbearable for his tired ass to stay around. " They reach out their hands for him to hold. He accepts their warm gesture and thanks them profusely.

" Believe me, I think I'm *REALLY* going to need that, he can be incessant! "

Another of the girls in the group comes forward. " Trust me, you were AMAZING! You certainly showed him you're no pushover. You took no shit, and, I hope this doesn't come across as patronising cos I don't know you, but I was *so* proud you! "

" Thank you so much. You girls are so cute.. So what are you going to be singing today? "

" Well, it's funny you ask that, because we're singing a relationship ending song. I Hate This Part by the Pussy Cat Dolls."

" Amazing song choice ladies, I really hope I get to hear you sing it, that song gives me chills. " He looks at the girls and smiles warmly. " How rude of me, I haven't even introduced myself.. I'm Theo, it's lovely to meet you? "

" I'm Tia and this is Monique. This lady here is Aisha, Rochelle at the back and Janine at my side and believe me when I say, it's a pleasure Theo. "

" I'm soooo relieved I'm next to you girls for this impossibly long, drawn out process. "

" Us too, you have saved us from the lecherous straight guys who keep trying to wink and flirt with us... It ain't going to happen, and they just don't seem to get it! " Monique says slightly too loudly.

Theo leans in and whispers. " Well, let's face it, that's men all over. You could tell them no a million times over and they still hear yes loud and clear. "

" What's crackin' man? " A voice says from in front of the girls.

Monique look at Theo and points subtly back at the new voice, gesturing that he's one of the guys trying it on with them.

The short, yet well built man continues to talk to Theo. " Sound like you having man trouble? I' kick his ass for you if need be? No man deserves that kinda shit, from anyone. "

" Thanks guys, but I'm okay, I'm old enough and ugly enough to handle him.... But when he gets here, if he is too much to handle I may change my mind. "

The guys look at each other and smile. " We get it. There are eight of us and one of him, what he goin' do? " They say reassuringly.

They all talk for what feels like thirty minutes or so, until out of nowhere they notice a disturbance at the rear of the queue. Out of the crowd emerges Andrew, red faced and out of breath.

Theo looks at the state of him, scarlet patches on his neck to match his face." No surprises then.. you look exactly the same as the night I walked in on you you prick! "

" Theo, give me a break! Are you really that perfect? Do you genuinely think you are that great. That special? You didn't think this would happen to you? You're gay for fucks sake! Of course you'll end up fucking someone, or get fucked over at some point or another. "

The group of girls look at him in shock and shake their heads in disgust.

Andrew hearing the tuts, retaliates in their direction. " No dick, no opinion! "

Aisha rebuttals focusing on his groin. " If that's the case, *why you still talking!?* "

Theo, still reeling from Andrew's previous comment says." Did you just do what I *think* you just did? Did you just categorise and stereotype *EVERY* gay man in one fell swoop? Fuck you you cunt! *I'm real, I* know how important monogamy is. I know the rewards of being with *one* man until the end of time... Maybe you are just too pathetic to understand how amazing it can be to have the definitive love of your life. Did you ever consider for one minute that you had found *your* everything when you had me? "

"Oh, enough with the drama Theo, this is nothing like you at all!!! "

Theo laughs, puzzled by his stupidity. " Until you walk in on your ' little miss thing ' licking out a girl, don't you *dare* tell me I'm being dramatic! "

"What's got into you?" Andrew says frowning.

Monique chirps in. " Clearly not you, loser. "

Andrew looks back at the girls, his face full of venom. " *What is this?? You don't know me, and you don't know him either !* "

" Believe me, I've heard enough to *know* I'm thankful I don't know you! "

One of the guys in front shouts down. " Yeah mate, your shit is tired, move it along! You're bringing Theo down, and he don't deserve none of this.. He needs a real man in his life. A real brother! "

Theo seizes his opportunity to mention Kez. He looks in the direction of the guy and puts his hand up. " It's funny you say that. I actually have already replaced him with a kind, strong, beautiful man, who *knows* what he's got when he's with me. Someone who I can adore and fall in love with and know that it's not a waste of time. "

The crowd groans with a unified ' boom' followed by laughter and clapping.

" Bullshit! You don't expect me to believe that for one second. You're so full of crap! " He says dismissively.

Unbelievably and unexpectedly, yet perfectly timed, Kez's arms appear to materialise from behind and wrap around him.

Theo jumps, almost scared to look around. *NO WAY! This can't be real?!* He forces as natural a smile as humanly possible considering the situation. *But, I couldn't dream this up if I tried.* He looks down at his waist to make sure the arms he feels encasing him, are in fact real.

" Hey my sweet baby, I'm so sorry that it took me so long to get here, the traffic was a nightmare. " Kez leans in to kiss his cheek and whispers in his ear. "*I have a really good memory. Last night, your friend Callum mentioned the time and place.* "

Theo's tension filled body relaxes, safe in the knowledge that there was a logical reason for how he knew to find him.

" That's okay honey, I'm just glad you're here. " He says smiling, relishing every second of this sweet revenge.

" Wow! Talk about an upgrade Theo! Shit! I'll even go as far as saying I'm kind of glad that asshole cheated on you Hun. " Says Monique, transfixed on the man now attached to him.

Holding Theo so tightly and lovingly, Kez smiles at the mass of people all watching the events unfold in front of them. " Hey everyone, how are you all doing? I think it's going to be a long wait , no? How are we going to pass the time? Anyone here know how to sing? "

The crowd laugh exaggeratedly, partially to show acceptance of he and Theo and partially because of his awful joke.

" Damn Theo! " says the stocky guy who had previously spoken to him in support. " I'm straight as a nail, but you are one beautiful looking couple. "

Andrew stands dead still in one place, unable to utter one word for a few moments. Eventually he speaks, visibly wounded. " How could you have done this already? We broke up a few days ago?! "

" Easily, actually. " Theo turns to face him. " It's like I said to you on the first date we had. If you cheat on me, you're invisible to me. In fact, can somebody hear that noise? " He pretends not to see Andrew. " It's kind of whiney and annoying, anyone else getting that? "

Aisha looks around, feigning to not see him too. " You know what Theo, I do hear that noise. It's starting to get on my fucking nerves actually. " She switches from aimlessly looking around to looking Andrew dead in the face. " *I really wish it would just go away.* "

" I don't hear it Aisha, " Says Monique, " but I do smell something disgusting in the air coming from that direction. " She says pointing at Andrew.

" Fuck you all, I'm done with this. You'll regret this one day Theo! " He says tearfully.

" I very much doubt that... Have you seen him? " He says cheerfully, pointing up and down at his new man.

The whole crowd erupts gleefully watching the broken man walk away before they all go about their business, practicing for their auditions.

Kez turns Theo around to face him, one hand cupping under his chin. " Are you okay love? "

" I'm elated.. Thank you for giving me the ammunition I needed to blow his brains up against the wall like that. It felt.. Thank you. "

" For you, almost anything. " He jokes.

Theo kisses him passionately and then says. " So, how long do I have the completely unexpected pleasure of being with you? "

" Let's see, I'm due to be lazing around on the sofa at two, going to the gym at four and then realising I don't want to, and finally pleasuring myself whilst thinking about being inside your beautiful ass at five... So, in essence nothing. You have me for the whole day baby."

" Stop it! You're going to turn me on. " Theo says adjusting himself.

" So, what do you want to do to pass the time whilst we wait for your audition? Judging by the queue it's going to be about ten o clock at night. "

Theo takes a moment, enjoying every second of Kez's embrace, his hot breath and general warmth radiating into him.

" I know what I want to do. " Theo says wrapping his arms around Kez's neck. " I want to get to know you. "

" Well, I think we know each other pretty well already. " He says squeezing his ass as a reminder.

" No silly! I mean seriously, you and I don't know much. Like basic stuff. Do we? First of all, I don't even know what you do for a living? "

" Take a guess. " He says stepping back and pointing towards his red leather jacket and his tennis bracelet and white gold chain.

" Ummmm do you work in a hospital? " Theo says sarcastically.

" If I did, I'd be giving you mouth to mouth everyday, whether you needed it or not. " He smiles warmly and squeezes Theo.

" Nah, I own a couple of stores in London. One is a men's jewellery and accessory store, the other is a men's fashion shop, specialising in leather and suede jackets.

" Well, that makes total sense, you rock the look, and you suit the bling. " He says feeling so lucky to be there in the sunshine with the beautiful man he has become close to.

" So how about you baby? What do you do? "

" So isn't this weather gorgeous? " Theo says attempting to change the subject.

" Theo... Come on, tell me. Unless I'm mistaken, wasn't it you a few minutes ago saying we should get to know each other. "

Okay, okay, point taken. I work in a bar, I know, it's boring, generic... Yawn! "

" That's cute baby, I like a man who knows his liqueur. "

" It's probably the most obvious, generic thing ever for someone to do in London for a living, but I make a killer Long Island ice tea though. "

" There is nothing like a good cock-tail. " He kisses Theo and looks into his eyes so deeply.

" This is kind of embarrassing, but I don't even know how old you are T? " He says wincing slightly.

" Don't worry, we haven't told each other.. What with all the kissing, cuddling, and you sticking yourself inside me at every given moment, we just never got around to saying. " He says bending down to do his shoe laces up, intentionally giving Kez the reminder of his rear.

He returns to his original position, reaching for Kez's hand. " I'm thirty one, how about you? "

" Thirty five here. " He says interlocking his fingers with Theo' s.

"So, apart from singing with more soul than any white man I've ever heard, what else do you like to do for fun my sweet one? "

" I'm quite ordinary really, I love the usual things, movies, music, obviously. Oh, and I really love to cook. "

" Wait a minute, Not only do you sing like an angel, make me laugh and make love beautifully, you also know how to cook.. I'm about three seconds away from asking you to marry me! So, give me something to bring me back to earth.. Bad points please. Don't hold back, we all have them."

" I have been known to serial kill men who cheat on me. " He says with half a smile.

" Oh really! So why isn't Andrew dead now? " Kez says, playing along.

" Ahhh well you see if I didn't have an audience in front of me, there would be a bullet planted firmly in his head right about now. " He says straight faced, dead pan.

" Well it's a good thing you're a serial killer, cos now I don't feel bad about telling you I'm a vampire. "

" Hmmm interesting, you don't see a lot of black vampires these days. You know, what with the pale skin traditional types. "

" You make me laugh so much babe. " He stares at him in adoration. " I don't think I'll ever forget the first time I saw you in the restaurant.. You completely took my breath away. "

He grabs Theo tightly, looks deeper into his eyes and opens his mouth, scared and emotional before uttering the words. " I know it sounds crazy, but I think I'm falling in love with you. You mean more to me than you'll ever know Theo. You are NOTHING like the guys I've been with before, you are just out of this world. "

Theo tries to avoid his stare, scared that he might say the same thing back to him. " I think you're amazing too Kez, but we are rocketing along at breakneck speed, so naturally, it frightens me how much I like you. I know myself well and I feel the .."

" Theo! Theo Morrison? You're next up! " A man with a headset and clipboard grabs him and leads him towards the entrance. Theo looks back at Kez, annoyed at the bad timing, as he is ushered away to the double doors in the distance.
" If you'd like to take a seat here, somebody will be in to take you through. "
He waits, feeling anxious, mainly down to the way things were left with Kez. *Deep inside all I wanted to do was tell him that I love him too. Now that decision has been taken away from me, for now. Perhaps it's for the best after all, with all the romance of Kez sweeping me off my feet, saving me from Andrew, it might just seem too perfect.* His thoughts are interrupted again.

" Theo, I'm sorry that we had to bring you down here. " A woman dressed in a striking blue power suit, much the same type Maria would wear for work, walks up to him.
" I'm sorry, I don't understand. " He says off guarded.
" Sorry, I'm being cryptic, let me explain myself. My name's Vanessa, I work at the label. You didn't *need*

to come down because we already saw your audition, and we loved you."

" Once again, I'm really confused. How have I auditioned when I haven't even opened my mouth?! "

She smiles and shakes her head. " I bet Callum didn't tell you, did he? "

" Tell me what? I'm really lost?! " He says, now starting to giggle at the absurdity.

" We saw you last night, Callum invited us down to see you. I'm guessing he didn't want you getting nervous so didn't tell you he set it up. Theo, you worked the crowd and you sounded *phenomenal*... You're in our top three. We'll be in touch soon. "

CHAPTER 9

Maria looks at her black Gerjot Madison jacket and Manhattan dress hanging in her wardrobe. It's classic pinstripe design and black silky material, reminding her why she bought it in the first place. It screams power and success which is precisely what she needs right now in light of the unknown status of her current employment. She takes out the two part outfit, brushes them down and tries them on. Relieved that it still fits, she takes a controlled breath and thinks of the interviews her sister has arranged for her today. Out of the two potential jobs, she focuses her attention on the catering job. To be given the opportunity to be able to showcase her talents on the scale it was always supposed to be, was overwhelming. Few people knew that Maria had become a formidable cook soon after leaving university. She had quite by luck, fallen into the world of fine cuisine whilst taking the Cordon Bleu certificate at Tante Marie. She had displayed such an aptitude of elegance and flair within her food presentation, coupled with an acute skill of balancing every herb and spice flawlessly. So much so that she was encouraged and supported by her father to work her way up until she was taking the CTH Level 4 Diploma in Professional Culinary Arts. She reminisces at the proud moment she graduated and beams to herself. *You can do this girl. You know you can.* As she gets more and more excited, she can visualise exactly what she would be serving up to them. She would start with a selection of tapas, including her chickpea, sherry vinegar, and chorizo stew. Her spicy potatas bravas, chorizo in red wine and meatballs in almond sauce. Stimulated by the culinary thoughts racing through her brain she recalls her back catalogue of equally impressive dishes. She could wow them with her dim sum and sushi, pork sumai, aubergine in harusame dressing, and chicken katsu. The mere mention of the food making her tastebuds well up with saliva. *How have I forgotten my love of the gastronomy? I used to lovingly prepare meal after meal in the past? Have I really become just another one of those people who get up in the morning and follow the standard nine to five? Have I really just thrown my life into a stress filled office environment for nothing?* She takes her deep purple Louis Vuitton bag and fills it will mascara, lip butter and various other things that she would need to protect herself from the blustery weather outside. She continues to think about the direction her working life has taken.

Why did I go for the job in the first place? True, I'm one of those lucky individuals that can turn their hand to both academic and creative, but the only true time I feel fire and passion for something is whilst I'm cooking or during sex. She smiles to herself, thinking about the previous night with Leon. She contemplates calling him, but decides against it when she rationalises how the conversation would go. He would ask her when they could next see each other and probably about half an hour in he would ask when they can be a unit again, and then eventually, the inevitable. The topic of conceiving and starting again where they last let off. She shudders and starts to feel hollow inside at the memory of the past experiences with him. Their loss and their grief amidst the destruction of their once loving relationship. *Could we really just pick up from where we left off? Is that even a feasible option? Then there's the question that neither of us want to ask ourselves again. Could IT happen again? Could life really be that cruel?* Of course the answer that comes back, every time, resounding louder in her subconscious is yes, it most definitely could happen again. *In all honesty, how could we cope with it this time? It wouldn't be easier just because we can prepare ourselves for that awful feeling of loss and mourning, it would be just be too hard to come back from and inevitably we would lose each other through the heartache.*

She takes a moment. *Why it is that I managed to get over the miscarriage so much easier than he did... Was it because I didn't really want a child as much as he had? Or was it the mere fact that I hadn't wanted the relationship that I had with him? Was I actually relieved that the tie that had once bound me to him was irrevocably broken? Was I settling for his comforting, masculine charms and his ability to make me feel like the woman I had secretly always wanted to feel? Vulnerable, cared for... Loved?*

Out of nowhere, she starts to feels the all too familiar emotion that she had felt for the majority of the past few days. " God damn Maria! Get a fucking grip! Surely there can't be enough saline left in your body to keep producing these tears!! " She says angrily to herself.She mops her eye with a tissue, and reconnects with her thoughts.

This time, she refocuses on a different subject. The date that she would be having tonight. Due to the tight schedule of the day, she knows that she will have to take a few extra accessories from her wardrobe to add to the ensemble to in-formalise her business like stance. She grabs the orange silk pashmina and her plunging crystal necklace along with a few other things and forces them into her already full bag.

She moves from the bedroom to the kitchen to obtain her own cookery book that she has consistently added to, year after year, containing all of her experimental culinary successes. She kisses it and holds it close to her bossom for a fraction too long. She makes a wish for success and the beginning of something amazing, something wonderful, something solid, something real. Before leaving her central london flat, she stares confidently out at the skyline and tells herself.

London is a place full of potential. I just need to grab it in the same way as I do my men.

The journey on the tube to South Kensington was an unwelcome reminder of everything she hated about travelling in London. She had forgotten how much she dreaded the suspicious looks given between strangers, the sea of unhappy, unfulfilled faces and the general lack of interaction people had with each other. On the rare occasions that she had seen a passenger speak to their friend or lover, they were only pleasantries. nothing real, nothing deep and meaningful. At times like this, she truly felt so thankful that she had found a friend like Theo. She had always known that he was her soulmate, her comfort blanket. He was her escape from the coldness and the anonymity that the city is known for.

In all the years that she had lived there, she had never hated London. She had just developed a jaded viewpoint of what it had to offer. There was no denying that the place was thriving with energy as a whole but the saddening truth is that when it is broken down into its individuals, it could only be described as an alienation nation.

As the tube reaches it's destination, she dismounts from the carriage. She makes her way through the oddly disconcerting warmth of the platform into the ever decreasing temperature of the world above.

She checks the satellite navigation application on her phone to locate the building where her first interview is due to take place. After a ten minute walk, eyes glued to the application, she hears the inevitable voice telling her that she has reached her destination. She takes a moment to look up and sees the regal looking signage, it's clean, defined lines intentionally intimidating as it powerfully rocks back and forth.

She notices the larger than life gay man buffing the already sparkling champagne flute on the counter and smiles openly.

" You look spectacular darling, I will make sure that Veronica is aware that you have greeted us with your fabulousness. " He says turning and strutting away in the most impressive statuesque nature.

Within minutes he reappears from the office above, smiling richly as a noticeably younger woman, with long and curly, fiery red hair, slowly follows behind him.

She looks at Maria, takes a step back and looks all around her before smirking mischievously. " Enchanté darling! You have the most incredible aura about you! I just want to lap your energy right up.... So do you practice at all? "

" Sorry, I'm not sure I understand. " She says baffled.

The woman shakes her hand and her head simultaneously.

" No need for *you* to apologise, it's *all me* darling. I do have a habit of getting ahead of myself without realising I need to let everyone else in as well! " She says laughing with her hand to her bosom. " What I meant to ask you, is do you believe in auras? You know, reading them, cleansing them. Just spirituality in general? "

This time concealing the confusion written across her face more successfully, Maria answers. " Oh I see! Umm I can't say that I have ever seen someone's aura, but I definitely believe in the overall energy you feel from someone when you meet them. "

" Splendid! That's good to know... Maria? Isn't it? " She says shaking her hand as she nods in acknowledgment. "Oh dear, I'm doing it again. I'm not explaining myself properly. You see, when I'm hiring someone, for any occasion, I invest in them as a person first and foremost. I guess the way I invest is rather unique, but I make ninety percent of my judgement and belief of a person on their spiritual strength and most importantly, on their auras. Hence the reason why I already know from seeing yours, that you have a great work ethic. You are hardworking, good natured, organised and it's abundantly clear to me that when you cook food, every stage is prepared lovingly from *your* soul to the dishes you breathe life into." She says admiring every inch of the exterior of Maria's being.

Maria stands perfectly still and smiles nervously. " Thank you.."

" In other words, you were born to do this darling and that's why this interview doesn't have to take place. I'd like to put you on the books immediately, and I'd love for you to do this charming school reunion that I think will suit you down to the ground. Correct me if I'm wrong, but I detect that you have strong roots to the countryside. I'm thinking the south west.. Somerset, by any chance? "

" Fuck! I mean, shit, sorry, wow! *How are you doing this??* Am I on one of those television shows where someone has told you everything about me, and then suddenly a drama develops and tests the poor clueless victim? "

Veronica laughs out loud, completely understanding Maria's surprised and shocked face. She takes her hand. " You and I are going to get along just wonderfully darling, I can just feel it. "

Maria relaxes in the knowledge that she now has a new job, and so soon after her epic suspension. It didn't matter to her how the strange, yet charming lady in front of her was managing to do what she was doing, she liked her.

" Thank you so much for this opportunity Veronica, I promise I won't let you down. " She says willingly.

" I already *know* you won't Maria." She says as they walk to her office. A mini waterfall structure and some Asian influenced statues and ornaments lay strategically around her office giving the place it's zen like qualities. " Right, so here are the basic requirements of this particular job. Firstly, the guest list followed by the known likes, dislikes and food allergies listed alongside their names. The quantity of food required for the people that will be there if full capacity is reached, including the allocation of potential partners, lovers, or random dates. The budget we have to stick too, the address of the venue in Crewkerne, the school having the reun- " She stops when she sees Maria's face turn pale as a ghost.

" You aren't going to believe this, but this is the school that my best friend went to ! " Maria says, unbelieving her own words.

Veronica smiles, bemused yet delighted by the news. " I never thought I would be saying this, but that's a *little* spooky. Even for someone like me. I guess this job *really* has been made for you darling. "

Maria nervously laughs, reading the list of guests allergies and their food likes and dislikes. She stops dead and stares at the list again when she sees a more than familiar name.. Kieran Jameson. Looking twice, then three times, she frantically looks at the rest of the guests... Jamie Saunders, Philip Reneé, Gemma Harold and then, there it was, clear as day. Theo Morrison.

" What is it dear? You look like someone's just walked over your grave? " Still no answer from Maria. " Now I'm guessing they're stamping up and down in it. "

" I'm so sorry, but I can't comprehend this! This is not just the school my best friend attended.. *This is actually his school year reunion!* "

" Well, you can't deny that your energy has *definitely* brought you to my little business. You get to see the people he talked about whilst he was growing up. What a lovely feeling that must be! "

" Exactly, and I'm pretty sure he must not have got the invite because he would have told me about it." She says

choosing not to mention to her new employer that she would love the opportunity to put laxatives into Kieran's food, the one boy who had bullied Theo mercilessly for years.

The overtly camp man from earlier knocks on the office door and enters, interrupting her thoughts.

" Veronica, your daughter is here to see you, she seems quite distressed."

" Oh no! Whatever is the problem? " She says concerned.

" Well, put it this way, she is standing in the reception area in full wedding attire and she does *not* look happy. "

" Oh no! Not another thing not going to plan in her wedding! At this rate she'll be wanting a divorce before she's even married. " She looks over at Maria. " I'm so excited we found you today, you little treasure. Now you have the plans, take them on, work your magic. We will discuss and reconvene end of the week? " She hastily shakes Maria's hand and walks out the office, turning briefly to say. " Jared could you show this wonderful lady out. "

He smiles warmly at her but blocks the doorway. " I think we should go out the back way, believe me you don't want to see her daughter in that dress. "

" Wow! Is it that bad? On a scale of one to ten, how bad does it look.

He looks both ways before saying. " Put it this way, it looks like a swan has just exploded all over her. "

" Oh my! What a duckastrophy! " Maria says covering her mouth to stop herself laughing.

" I know, it's almost as much of a train wreck as the husband to be. He looks like one of those types of guys who loves his mum a little too much if you know what I mean. " He says leading her out of the office, unconventionally arm in arm.

" Brings new meaning to keeping it in the family I guess. " Maria says, feeling comfortable in her new acquaintances company.

" Exactly! Well, I'm sure I'll be seeing a lot more of you over the next few months Maria. Take care, safe journeying. " He turns, checks his reflection in the office window, before walking back in.

An eight minute journey on the Piccadilly line later, and Maria once again resurfaces into the busy hustle and bustle of The West End, ten minutes early for her rendezvous with Theo.

She walks up Shaftesbury Avenue, turns into Great Windmill Street and there on the left, just after St. James's Tavern, is Grace Bar. The rich, muted purple front surround of the building, indicating decadence and style, whilst the slightly weathered wooden doors, somewhere between beech and cedar, give the place an approachable, inviting feel.

She enters and scans the bar, looking for Theo. She walks towards the bar, her eyes drawn to the intricately detailed wooden eagle perched high above in the centre of the wall behind. The two ornate mirrors on either side creating perfect symmetry amongst the multitude of wines and spirits. The tables and stools, deep walnut in colour give the place a masculine energy that instantly lifts when the softness of the ample bohemian crystal chandeliers hanging above, intertwine. She sees Theo sat on the luxurious dark brown booth, book ended on each side with a white metal floral divider, waving frantically in front of her. He gets up to hug her as she climbs the step to join him.

" *I got the job Theo! I got the job!* " She says animatedly.

He smiles widely. " Okay, fuck the virgin mojito' s, let's get some tequila shots because we *both* have something to celebrate.. " He pauses for dramatic effect. " *I'm in the top three for the auditions!* "

Maria screams unrestrained. " Clearly you meant a bottle of tequila, not a shot, right?! *That's incredible*

T! " She says hugging him again. " I guess, we shouldn't get too drunk, really. I mean, isn't that what we'll be doing *once* our disaster blind dates are over with? " Maria says taking a sip of Theo's non alcoholic drink.

" Speak for yourself sis, I already know mine's a hunk! " He says laughing loudly. " Seriously though, I think it actually makes *more* sense to be a blithering, drunken idiot as the painful attempt at chit chat ensues making me want to stick needles in my eyes. " He finishes the drink in preparation for the onslaught of alcohol. " Remind me Hun, why are we going on these dates again? "

" Well, I know why I am, but as for you, I have no idea why you don't just call mister handsome and invite him instead. He is so lovely Theo, and he's gorgeous, and I can tell he's *crazy* over you. "

" I know, I know... Believe me I know! " He says getting his wallet out to buy the first round. " When I'm with him, I swear I can hear romantic songs playing. He is just a dream come true, but it's just too terrifying, isn't it? Or am I just being stupid? "

" You're being stupid Theo, now let's get fucked. "

" Bitch!"

" I'm kidding, of course you're not being stupid, you're just building up a little wall around the house of you. "

" Alright guru Martinez, where did that come from? "

" I don't know, I'm just saying that I think you need to *let go* with this guy. He's tailor made for you. "

" He definitely does *suit* me. " He says, pretending to think his own joke is funny.

" What's the worst that can happen? In light of recent events, I think we can both safely say that that has already happened. Also, I know you hun. This is not like you, you don't hold grudges. You move on with a smile on your face. So, I know it's not all about the Andrew bisexuality thing, so what is it? "

He takes a sit back in the chair to think about what she has just said. " I never gave much time to think about it before, but you are right. I could see that he and I were coming to the end of the relationship, and it's not about the betrayal, especially since I had my revenge yesterday. "

" Sooo what do you think it is it? "

" I think it's because I like Kez so much, that the idea of potentially losing him makes me not want to get involved with him in the first place. "

" Bingo, that adds up, " She says sitting back too, crossing her legs in an analytical way. " but you do realise, now that I know this, I am not going to let it go. You *need* to talk to him about this. "

" Ok, I will, after our date tonight. " He says playfully.

" You don't have to go on it you know Theo, the whole reason I wanted you to do it, is to get you out there again, but if you are going to see what happens with Kez- "

" If you honestly think I'm going to let my best friend potentially get raped by a non faced stranger, you'd better think again. "

" Well if you're sure, then great. "

" Of course I am. It's you and me against the world, it doesn't wash if the double act becomes a single act. "

They continue to talk and drink virgin cocktails for the afternoon as they discuss each other's successes from the previous day and today well into the early evening. It was only when a passing couple mentioned that they were so relieved it was happy hour, that they realise it is seven o clock and that they would be meeting their respective dates any moment now.

" Shit! How's my makeup T? "

" You look like a max factor advert, trust me. He will be so intimidated by your beauty, he probably won't even be able to get it up for you, you're *that* hot. "

" Don't say that! " She yelps.

"I know Hun, I know.. I'm kidding, it's- " He looks towards the entrance to the pub, signifying that he's seen a new person entering. " Huh, how funny...Guess who's here? "

" *Who*? " She says scared to look up.

" It's Reuben, and...*oh my god! He's wearing the colours that your blind date said he would be wearing!!* "

" *You're fucking kidding me! Please tell me you're joking like that time you said you had got drunk and slept with the really grotesque guy at the local chippy who picks his nose?!* " She says petrified.

" I'm *dead* serious, and I'm afraid to say it, but he's clocked that it's you who's his blind date. So we can't even escape now.. Okay, he's walking over. I'm going to go and sit on the opposite booth and wait for my own personal disaster to turn up. You'll be fine Hun, I'm only over there. "

" Well, this is awkward as hell! In fact this is more uncomfortable than going for my first smear test! " She says as he approaches the table.

Reuben, head hanging sheepishly, speaks. " Yes I hear you. I'm the same, I'd rather have a prostate exam right now than do this. " He hesitates before uttering. "In all seriousness, do you want me to go? I would completely understand if you did. "

" No Reuben, we both *really* need a drink right now. So we may as well do that together instead of drinking alone in our respective houses. Rioja or Merlot ? " She says pointing to the bottles on the table that she and Theo had only just ordered moments before Reuben had walked in. He picks up the bottles and looks at the labels on each.

" Oh, we have that in common." She says biting her lip.

" What do you mean? "

" I just saw you checking out the percentages. "

" No I wasn't, I was looking at the variety of grape and the country of origin and... Okay, you got me, I'm all about the percentage. Let's face it, after what has happened tonight, we need to get off-of-our-faces drunk. "

Reuben opens the bottle and fills both glasses to the very brim. They both lift their glasses and toast. " So, about the suspension. I feel so bad about it Maria, you do know I had no choice. If I could, I would have loved to have swept it under the carpet. Forget that it had happened and move on, but it was impossible because every fucker in that place had a copy of it via email. That fucking bastard Chris! " He says unexpectedly.

" Umm okay, are you alright there Rueben? I mean, you do understand that it wasn't *you* that was in that video with your cock out, yes? "

" Of course I do! I just hate it when men take advantage of women in that way, and especially when it's you.. It just hurts me. "

Maria takes a big mouthful of the Rioja and plays with her hair nervously. " What do you mean especially when it's you? I'm a little confused. "

He looks down into his glass fumbling the base of it. " Well, you can't tell me you didn't know that I've always had a thing for you. "

She picks up her glass and knocks the contents back. " If the way you behaved towards me, was the way you behave to someone you find attractive, *how on earth do you behave to someone you despise?* "

" What? You had no clue. " He says, genuinely shocked.

" Even Mensa members wouldn't have picked up on that Reuben! I actually thought you hated me! "

Reuben laughs uncontrollably. He finally stops and shakes his head, still smiling. " Oh dear! I guess this is why I've been single for what feels like forever, then? I really don't know women do I? "

Maria reaches out her hand and grasps his. " You might need a *little* bit of help. "

He looks at her and stares cluelessly.

" Okay, you might need a *lot* of help. "

" I think we might need a few more bottles of this for tonight. " He says standing up and making his way to the bar.

Maria smiles to herself as her phone beeps. It's Theo, the message reads :

' I knew I was right. '

She looks over at him, puzzled. Another beep, this time a picture message. It was of her a few moments previous to the first text. She was smiling to herself, content and hopeful.

She looks over at him, and sticks her middle finger up at him, then texts him back.

Theo reads the text. ' Where is yours? ' He takes a few moments before he texts her back. He tells her that he has cancelled on him but that he's more than fine with it. He adds that he is going to stay for a few more drinks and make sure she is okay.

Just at that moment, Reuben reappears with a few more bottles of wine.

" This enough, do you think? "

" Pretty sure this will have the same effect as a tranquilliser dart on us. "

" Oh! see I call this my usual Friday night. " He says straight faced until he sees the horror on her face. " I'm joking , I couldn't possibly drink this much... I guess I'm not just useless with women, I'm also unfunny as well. "

Maria laughs, relieved that he was kidding. " No, okay, Its *me*, I need to relax. This is a *very* unusual situation to be in and I'm probably coming across as being a right bitch, which I'm sorry about. " She takes a deep breath. " Okay, let's just talk. "

" I can do that, I think. " He says looking adoringly at her.

" So, can I ask you Reuben, why are you feeling you need to be on a dating site to meet women? You're clearly a handsome man, you have a great job, you're self sufficient and I'm assuming living on your own, no? Or are you going to disappoint me and tell me you're living with your mum? "

" All of the above Maria.. Except the mum thing, I'm definitely not Norman Bates. " He looks at her inquisitively. " Can I ask you that very same question back? Why a dating site, you're beautiful .. There isn't one guy in that office who's tongue isn't lacking moisture by the time you walk by. "

" Does that include you Reuben? " She says cheekily.

He stops to think, debating on whether to confide. " You know when I meet up with you for meetings, or catch ups? "

" Uh Huh, yep. "

He shifts in his chair uncomfortably, taking a large swig of the strong wine. " Have you ever noticed that I always have a book, or clipboard with notes on them, in front of my nether region? "

" *No!* "

" Yes, that's the reason. I would take out someone's eye if I didn't hold that bad boy down! " They both erupt with laughter, partly from the revelation, and partly from the alcohol.

" You know that whole dumping Chris thing. Well, it was because of one big reason... Or should I say, *small* reason.."

Reuben nods, putting the pieces together of the puzzle. " Ah, I *see*.. Is that why you reached out for his hand to direct him? "

" Exactly! Do you thing I would normally take fingers over fucking? "

The familiar sound of the door opening and closing temporarily distracts Maria.

" You sneaky little shit! " She says out loud.

" Sorry? What was that? What did I do wrong?? "

" Not you Reuben..Theo! My best friend."

" I'm confused as hell? Have I really drank that much that I don't even understand English now? "

Maria looks over at Theo who is smiling and shrugging. He stands up and warmly hugs the man who has walked through the door. There, stood opposite, was Kez beaming from ear to ear.

CHAPTER 10

" I'm really glad you called me, Theo." He says taking his hand in his. " I was a little worried about the way we were interrupted so abruptly yesterday at such a crucial time. " He waits for Theo to acknowledge his emotional out pouring and then remembers the reason for him not being able to answer yesterday. " Oh shit! How rude of me! How did it
go? "

Theo holds up three fingers and smiles.

" Baby that's amazing! Down to the last three? I knew you could do it. "

Theo, seeing the look in Kez's eyes, re-addresses his original question. " Just so you know, I'm really glad I called you too. There was something I wanted to tell you that afternoon. I really shouldn't have hesitated before that guy ushered me off to the audition room. I tried to call you last night but you weren't picking up.
"

Kez's face drops a little. " I'm sorry about last night. I was meaning to call you back but things were a little busy, and I - "

" You don't have to explain anything at all. What I was going to say is that, " he takes a deep breath. " I feel the same way. I feel like I'm falling in love with you too. I've just been too scared to say anything because, well, because it's you. "

" Because it's me? "

" Yes because it's *you.* "

" Last time I checked it was me! " Kez touches his chest and stomach theatrically. " Well, I hope it's me?! " He says laughing before grabbing Theo's hand again.

" What I'm trying to say, and failing miserably at, is that being with you scares me because we have so much fun. You're *so* kind, *so* loving, *so* romantic.. In fact it's easier to say what you *aren't.* "

"*I know Theo, I won't hurt you baby.* When I said that you are everything I look for, I meant it. Us making it to the end. " He says rubbing Theo's hand. " I can see it now, both there on our deathbeds. Your hand in mine as we both disconnect each other's life support machines and leave our crusty old decrepit bodies to fester away. "

Theo laughs at the image. " How romantic?! "

" Okay, maybe that was a little bit morbid. " He thinks for a second, then begins again. " How about this, we will be together until one of us has to be spoon fed every meal and have their incontinence pants changed by the other..."

" Yes, that's a whole lot better. Living like we *should* be dead as opposed to *actually* being dead. "

He pulls his chair closer to Theo, touching his face and says.

" This time I've definitely got it... How about we just stay together.. Full stop. We continue to look forward to every moment we have. We relish every embrace, every intense moment of lovemaking, every time we laugh, or cry-. "

" With happiness of course? " Theo cheekily interjects.

" Because living with me will only ever be a happy experience. Plus if I'm ever mad with you, you would have had to have done something so terrible, and that's not something that you would do, is it dearest? "

" It all depends. " He let's go of his hand for a second and sits back into his chair, looking smug. " What is your personal definition of terrible, Theo? Then I will know if I'm going to be setting up residence permanently in the spare room or not? "

" Well, let me think. The toilet seat being left up, dirty clothes left on the floor, crumbs on the sofa, not making the bed.The list goes on..." He says counting on his fingers in jest. " No, not really.. Those things do annoy me, but the only things that would be instant deal breakers would be cheating...cheating, oh and cheating, and don't let me forget cheating. "

" Right, gotcha. So *lying* to you is not an issue then? " He says smiling broadly.

" Alright, you make a very good point, lying is another big no no. How about you? What are the things you cannot live with in a partner? "

" Someone who doesn't give up his ass when I'm horny. "

Theo chokes on his drink. " Seriously Kez! I really want to know. "

" Okay, okay. " He pretends to think. " Someone who won't suck my dick when I'm horny. "

Theo laughs and shakes his head. " You really are easy to please aren't you? Those are hardly unreasonable demands. I mean my ass is open to you like a twenty four hour Tesco and my mouth has more suction than Dyson's latest vacuum cleaner. "

" Don't I know it. I have no complaints there at all. You are incredibly good at the nasty, but in all honesty, my deal breakers are the same as yours. No lying and no cheating just openness and honesty at all times. "

As the two of them look into each other's eyes, they start to truly realise how amazingly well connected they are. They continue to talk freely, all the while being tactile, rubbing fingers and locking legs under the table.

Theo's gaze is momentarily disturbed by the sound of Maria's laugh echoing through the bar. He watches her as she too, is holding her dates hand, and not unwillingly either. In fact she was displaying higher levels of affection than he has ever seen her do before in the whole time he has ever known her. He coughs loudly to grab her attention.

Maria looks over at him and scowls light heartedly, and then looks back at Reuben.

" Something wrong Maria? " He says squeezing her hand a little tighter.

" No, not at all. My friend Theo over there, looked like he might have need a lozenge for his throat, but then I realised he won't be needing any extra throat lubrication tonight after all. " She says loud enough for him to hear her.

Reuben, seeing the two men clearly fixated on each other, smiles and waves at them in acknowledgement.

" They look like a cute couple, how long have they been together. "

" About five minutes, but you wouldn't know it by the way they behave. Trust me, it makes me so much happier knowing that he is out there enjoying himself after his whole ex situation. You know, he's the reason I'm on this blind date in the first place? "

" I should be shaking him by the hand then because I was actually dreading it until I saw that it was actually you. "

She thinks for a second before drunkenly confessing. " Did you know that I have always had a crush on you too? "

" You're joking with me aren't you? Just teasing, no? "

" No honestly, when I first started working at the firm I could not stop looking at you! "

" Really? Me? " He says flabbergasted. " I didn't notice. "

She crosses her legs, and arms pretending to be offended.

" Well that was until after the millionth time of me coming into the office and pushing my breasts in your face, and getting no positive reaction. That's when I decided to let it go. "

" Ah see, I thought that was just you! You know, just your sexual energy. " He struggles for the right words to say. " Your womanly-ness. "

" Womanly-ness? I'm sorry, did we just rewind back into the Victorian times? " Seeing him laugh, relaxes her further. " Is that even a word? Are you sure you were educated at Reading university? "

" I'm just saying you have an overtly sexual way about you, " He quickly adds. " which is great.. and obviously I love you. " Realising the wine has let his guard down momentarily. " I mean *like you*. "

" Wait a minute, back up. Did you just say *love*? " She looks into his face and sees the unmistakeable truth. The vulnerability clearly eating away at him.

" Maria, just.. Oh.. " He says, his words disjointed.

" *Ummm when did this happen? Christ! Now it's my turn to feel like the clueless kid in the classroom who hasn't figured out who just farted.* " She takes another gulp. " So, you *love* me? "

He nods his head silently.

Maria moves her chair around closer to him. His head now completely slumped into his chest. She puts her hand under his chin and lifts it gently until his eyes meet hers. She smiles warmly, giving him the affirmation he needs to take the lead. He leans in and joins his mouth with her warm, wine tinged lips and kisses her gently. Lingering kiss after kiss, they breathe unevenly, surprised by how amazing the simplest action has mesmerised them both completely.

Without thinking Maria blurts out. " *Please don't be bad in bed!* " She instantly covers her mouth. " I'm sorry, where did that come from?! " Realising how awful it must have sounded to say that, she explains. " It's just that you're such an amazing kisser. I just hope the rest of your skills match that. "

" I see, well only one way to find out.. But only if you want to, no pressure. I can still take you back to yours, or mine... your choice, entirely your choi- "

She stops him talking with her mouth and gives him the non verbal answer.

" I'll get the chauffeur to bring the car around. Are you okay to wait here for a bit Maria? " He stumbles as he stands.

She smiles at him and nods. He leaves the pub, looking back at her once, then twice, each time his smile growing more.

" Maria! Get your ass over here now! " Theo's voice booms drunkenly across the bar.

" What babe? " She says nonchalant.

" Did I, or did I not tell you, that you had a crush on him? "

" Alright smarty pants! How about you? Have you finally told this gorgeous man sitting in front of you that you are so into him, that your ass gets wet whenever he's around? "

Kez looks at Theo lustfully. " No he didn't, but now I do. "

" That's not the case! It's not every time.. *Maria! Seriously!* " He says chastising her.

" Lighten up Theo. You know I'm only kidding, I'm so relieved you both seem to be making a go of it. " She says taking Theo's head to her breasts. " By the way, have you actually looked in a mirror and seen how unbelievably adorable you look together? If you haven't, I suggest you do, you could be on the front cover of Attitude magazine, if they ever do an interracial special. "

They look at each other, captivated. Losing themselves in each other's eyes.

" Okay, don't do anything I wouldn't do. " She says as she sees Rueben re-entering the pub.

" *Trust me, that doesn't leave much.* " Theo whispers to Kez behind his hand.

" I heard that! " She says looking back over her shoulder as she leaves with her old boss.

" You were meant to sis! " He shouts after her.

" Right, I'm just going to drain the snake, back in a minute. " Kez says, giving Theo a fifty pound note as he heads towards the toilets. " Get whatever you want my love, I'll have a double gin and tonic. "

Theo heads to the bar, lightheaded from the alcohol, but dizzy with emotion. He orders the drinks and starts to piece the events of the past few days together in his mind. *Who gets this lucky? Who finds their soulmate so soon after getting rid of someone so soulless? If this was a movie playing right now, I would be cringing at the obviousness of the uncomplicated romantic leads. First of all, I would be refusing to believe this beautiful London based black man would be so totally enamoured by this one average looking white guy. Second of all, the fact that they fit so perfectly, both in the way they bounce off each other's humour, each other's emotional honesty, and if that isn't enough of a stretch of the imagination, you expect me to believe that the sex is completely on point. Flawless? No! It would just seem so fake. Yet here I am, living that very same fairy tale. Meeting mister right and falling in love in record time.*

" Hey Theo! " A vaguely recognisable woman's voice says behind him. He turns around to see the woman from the Excel centre who delivered the wonderful news of his successful audition. " How are you? I'm surprised your ears haven't been burning? "

Theo smiles open mouthed, genuinely pleased to see her.

" Why do you say that.. Vanessa wasn't it? "

" That's right, I'm Vanessa, and this is Daryl. " She introduces a tall, handsome black man with a striking resemblance to LL Cool J.

" I have to say you have been causing quite a stir in the office today. " She continues. " Your friend Callum brought in one of your CDs today.. You truly have a gift Theo! "

" Yeah Theo, you are awesome.. true talent, for real. " Darryl said with a strong New York accent that vibrated with bass.

" Which is why we don't want you to be in a top three audition for a manufactured solo artist where all your songs have been laid down already for you. We want to develop you as the artist you already are. Be that singer, or songwriter, or both. What do you say Theo, can you dig? "

" *Oh my god! Yes, yes! That sounds insane!* I'm completely, one million percent all in! " Theo screams just as Kez walks out of the toilets.

" Is everything okay here babe? " He says concerned.

Theo runs over to Kez, interlocking his hand with his.

" I'd like to introduce you to Vanessa, the woman who told me I was whittled down to the last three yesterday, and this is Daryl. "

" Hey, nice to meet you man. " Darryl booms. " I'm going to be Theo's music producer, slash engineer in the studio. "

Theo excitedly continues. " They want me to go in the studio.. record my own stuff! Callum gave them my CD... I'm so excited I think I might die if I don't calm down! "

The three of them laugh as Theo takes a seat by the bar. Kez grabs Theo and kisses him hard and passionately. " My baby is going to be making music again, I'm so proud of you T! "

Sensing it is time to leave the happy couple to enjoy the news, Vanessa starts to speak. " Perfect! Well, we only popped in to tell you that. It was Darryl that recognised you through the window as we walked by the place. "

Theo frowns. " Sorry, I don't want to sound rude.. But how did you know what I looked like? I haven't met you before, *have I?* I'm pretty sure I'm usually quite good with faces."

Daryl laughs and slaps his back. " You British guys crack me up! No, we haven't met.. officially, until tonight, but I was there last night too with Vanessa. She brought me along to see if I liked you and felt I could work with your vocals, and I have to admit, I was blown away.. Looks like the UK really does have some talent. "

Vanessa interrupts. " I have a really good feeling about this collaboration Theo, but we really must dash now.. Tomorrow at eight in the morning at Dean Street Studios, sound okay to you? "

Theo looks over at Kez. " Well, would it be okay if I stayed at yours tonight? It's just that the tubes at that time of the morning are hellish to get from Balham to Soho, whereas from your place, it's the shortest of tube trips? "

Kez puts his hand on Theo's head and caresses him. " Of course you can, you don't ever have to ask. You just need to make us breakfast in the morning, or else there will be trouble! You know what happened last time, don't make me have to use the frying pan on you again! " Seeing the horrified looks on Darryl and Vanessa's faces, he hastily adds. " Kidding! Promise I'm kidding, I'm not an abusive partner. It's just my dark sense of humour. "

" Domestic violence is never funny or clever for that matter, man. " Says Darryl solemnly.

" *Neither is wearing sun glasses when it's pitch dark outside, but you don't see me saying anything.* " He whispers in Theo's ear as he kisses his cheek.

" Peace man, we out. " He says pointing at Theo.

The two say their goodbyes and exit swiftly.

" Is it just me, or is ridiculous to say peace when someone' s leaving a room that clearly never had a war in it when they entered? " Kez says, visibly annoyed by Darryl's hasty judgement.

Theo chuckles. " I know, it really is nonsensical isn't it? "

" Oh, and don't get me started with the, ' We out. ' " Kez says mimicking Darryl. " No you're clearly not, because you're pretending to be with the girl you just walked in with! "

" Yes, he was definitely gay, wasn't he? You can always tell when a guy overcompensate with butch behaviour I mean, if he growled any more he would actually be a dog. "

They sit back down and continue to drink and talk.

" I feel bad for Vanessa though, she probably has no idea that when he's inside her, all he's thinking about is the latest porn video he's bookmarked on his favourite sex site. " Theo states, taking a sip of his Peach Mimosa.

" And I guarantee that he fucks her from behind so he doesn't have to accidentally touch her breasts. "

" Don't remind me. " An old memory enters Theo's head.

" What do you mean babe? I thought you hadn't had sex with a woman before? "

" I haven't, but I went out with a guy for a while who might as well have been. He had bigger boobs that Pamela Anderson. "

" I never had you pegged you as a chubby chaser T?! "

" I'm not! Believe me, he started off looking like 2 Pac and by the end of our relationship, he was More like twenty packs.. of lager!! "

Kez, removes the lime slice from his gin and tonic. " I can't say I've ever been with an overweight guy before. Most of them have been gym bunnies or slim types. "

" Well, I knew the time had come to finish with him, when one night, he was dreaming. It must have been of a sexual nature, because out of nowhere, he starts to climb on top of me."

" You do realise, in my head this guy you're describing, looks identical to Jabba the Hutt. "

" You know what, I think I'd have preferred that. " He recoils at the fat sweaty mess laying on top of him like a beached whale.

" Anyway, so I'm trying to wake him and nothing's working, and the more I try to wake him up, the more he grabs on tighter to me. "

" That's horrible Theo. I hate that you went through that. " He says sliding up next to him.

" I know! At this point all I can think about is the newspaper headline. ' Man suffocates accidentally in sordid sex act. ' "

Kez laughs at his humorous re telling. " In all seriousness, that must have been terrifying. How did you escape? "

" Well, luckily I remembered my diaphragm breathing I learnt from my singing lessons and managed to tighten my stomach muscles so he didn't crush me, and then I just used momentum. I rocked back and forth, until I rolled him off *me*..and *onto* the floor. I would *never* want someone like that ever again. I love that you are naturally masculine Kez, and even though you are the strong man you are, you aren't scared to kiss or cuddle me in public. "

" That's because I want to show the world how proud I am to call you my man. " He says grabbing Theo and pulling him close, kissing the back of his neck. " Besides that, with my height and my body type, nobody's *ever* going to have a problem with me kissing anyone I choose to. "

Theo melts into his embrace. " Is it wrong that I love it when you get all territorial on me baby? " He says snuggling back into him.

" Not at all, I love that you look to me for support. I love that you look at me like I'm the only man in the room. You always make me feel *so* special. " He says kissing him on the head.

" That's because you are special.. So special. Right, let's go back to yours, I'm needing some serious naked time with you. "

They finish their drinks and hail the nearest taxi. The journey passes quickly and before too long they are outside Kez's flat. The moment Theo steps out of the car, he is picked up and flung over Kez's shoulder.

" What are you doing? You crazy man. " He slaps his back repeatedly, laughing all the while.

Kez adopts a caveman voice as he searches for his keys. " You Theo..me Kez..me take you to bed..me fuck you. "

" Please! If you make me laugh any more, I won't be able to control my bladder. Unless you want a costly dry cleaning bill for your Versace leather jacket, I suggest you stop. "

" Okay, okay, I'll stop. " He opens the door to his flat, and still holding on to Theo, he climbs the wood and metal combination stairway, straight to his bedroom.

He flings him onto the plum velvet sheets and hangs his blue leather jacket on the cream door. The outline of his chiselled, powerful, muscular body against the backdrop of the well lit arched doorway, takes Theo's breath away. He pulls his white T-shirt off to reveal his incredible body, his white gold chain glimmering against his smooth black body.

Theo, although quite tipsy, fumbles to undress himself just before Kez slides himself onto the bed with him. He takes him in his powerful embrace and holds his back so tightly with one hand and the other on the back of his neck. He takes his tongue and licks his chest hungrily, working his way up to his neck and kisses him softly at first and then dominates his whole body with the weight of him. He pushes his legs back towards his chest to naturally open him up. Theo moans with anticipation at the inevitable penetration that was about to take place. In such a short time, he had grown to love the way that Kez felt when he filled him up with his perfectly sized dick. He remembered being amazed that Kez had instinctually known how to enter him. He knew exactly how to make him relax, how to open him up without any effort. Before long he was in familiar territory. He could feel Kez push himself inside him tenderly, the look on his face of pure ecstasy. Eyes closed at first, as the passion takes over him, then, within seconds he reopens them to look at Theo.

" You're so fucking beautiful baby, I want you to know how much I love being inside you. I love filling you up, and making you give in to me. Tell me how much you love it sexy. "

Theo let's out a moan. " Oh Kez, you're so incredible. I love feeling your pulsing, big black dick taking my tight white ass. "

Kez stops for a second, pleasantly surprised by Theo's dirty talk. " Wow, that is so fucking hot! I love that you love me overpowering you, taking that white ass of yours. You know it belongs to me, I own you T. "

Theo's dick, hard as rock, sends waves of pleasure through his brain, causing him to have mental eruption after mental eruption . He hungrily takes Kez's face in his hands. " I want to feel your tongue rape my mouth baby, you know I want every inch of you inside me. "

Kez, without thinking, and turned on so much by the sordid requests ebbing from Theo's mouth, rams his tongue deep in his throat, sweat dripping from his forehead. " I fucking love you Theo, I fucking love you more than I've ever loved anyone before. "

Theo wraps his legs around him, only taking his mouth away from his, to nibble on his earlobe and to lick the sweat off of Kez's forehead. " I love you to my sexy man. "

" You really are freaky aren't you T? I love that about you. "

Theo takes his hand away from his own dick to grab Kez's ass and pull him deeper into him. " I was born for you to make love to me baby. My ass might as well have your name all over it. "

" I can tattoo it in my own special way if you want? "

Theo returns to kissing his lips as he watches his lover's ass grind up and down, back and forth, as waves of pleasure come over him. He can feel himself getting close, as Kez hits his pleasure zones repeatedly, over and over again. Theo, unable to utter another word, erupts in ecstasy as simultaneously Kez let's out an almighty groan as he climaxes intensely.

" You are the most amazing lover... Ever! " Says Theo struggling for breath.

" I'll never let you go baby, as long as I am breathing, I'll never let go. " He says intensely holding him as they both fall into an exhausted deep sleep.

The next morning, the light shining through the curtains awakens Theo as yet another bright, yet cold autumnal day begins. He reaches out his arm to touch Kez, but instead his fingers are met with a folded over piece of paper with his name written on it. He takes a moment to focus his blurry eyes on the love note.

" My sweet baby, I had to get to work early and you were sleeping so peacefully, so I didn't want to wake you. There is food in the fridge, coffee freshly brewed, help yourself.. Have a great day in the studio. "

" Shit! The studio! Fuck I need to get my ass ready! "
Theo shouts as he stumbles blindly through the flat,
opening door after door randomly, until he sees the
blinding white walls of the bathroom. He closes the
door, and waits for his tired eyes to adjust to the
bright lime green wall jutting out to which the wet
room is attached. He takes the matching green terry
cloth towel off the back of the bathroom door, and
places it on top of the rectangular beech storage shelf,
before having a hot shower. The warmth of the heated
floor, pleasantly unsettles his senses due to the cold
appearance of the grey slate floor. He sees the
oversized, futuristic digital clock on the opposite
facing wall of the vast bathroom and sees that he has
plenty of time to make it to the studio in time. He
takes a rare, uninterrupted moment to practice his
scales, singing at the top of his voice, warming his
vocals to life.

He finishes his shower, and with far less
disorientation, locates the kitchen and pours himself
a coffee from the sleek, streamlined coffee machine.
He takes a moment to admire and appreciate the bold
purple gloss kitchen units, oozing style and screaming
of quality and confidence. In the centre of the room,
the island presented a selection of croissants, pain au
chocolat and breakfast buns, along with a jug of
freshly squeezed orange and pineapple juice. He eats
hungrily, thankful for the thoughtfulness, and the

food fuel he would be needing for the vocally challenging day ahead of him.

As he finishes eating, a thought stops him suddenly. *Damn! I didn't expect to be in the studio today, so I haven't got any clothes to wear!*

He walks back into the bedroom and rummages through the laminated mahogany chest of drawers and pulls on a pair of Kez's boxer briefs.

Thankfully our waist sizes are the same. On the other hand, I don't think I'll be lucky enough to find a t shirt that will fit me though, since I have such a small frame compared to Kez's wide shoulders.

He walks over to the matching wardrobe that nearly spans the entire wall and opens it. The feeling of déjà vu hits him with full force, rushing over him as his freshly consumed breakfast begins to resurface in his throat. There in front of him, hanging on every coat hanger, lay a woman's garment. His head begins to spin as he forces the second side of the wardrobe open. Confronted again by scatterings of more women's clothes, he lays back down on the bed, his heart literally bursting and breaking with every minute. He sobs uncontrollably, unable to move, paralysed. The realisation that the nightmare is happening all over again, lifts him to his feet. He runs to the bathroom just in time before the contents of his stomach surge into the toilet. It is only then, when he steadies himself whilst sitting on the toilet, that he sees the picture in the bathroom window ledge he had been oblivious to before. His boyfriend, cuddling into a woman.... and a child.

CHAPTER 11

Theo dries his eyes, his heart broken, his mind numbed. He reluctantly allows himself to think about how blissfully happy he had been moments before the discovery of the evidence of the woman living in his lovers flat. Yet with every happy memory that he recalls, he is faced simultaneously with the gut wrenching betrayal that had led him to lose everything in an instant.

He sobs inconsolably in the middle of the bed as his thoughts consume him. *How could this be happening again?? Surely this must be the cruelest trick ever pulled on one human being? This has to be the worst violation of trust between lovers that has ever existed. Not only has this very same thing happened to me days ago, Kez reassured me that the same scenario had befell him too! How could he lie so easily like that? He had explained in great detail how crushed he was to have discovered that his boyfriend was having a bisexual affair. Not only that, he had retold the whole story with tears in his eyes!* A shocking thought enters his head. *'What if the reason he could tell such a authentic story was because in actual fact, HE was the bisexual man who had cheated on HIS unsuspecting boyfriend! That it was he that had strayed from the innocent party who was so completely head over heels in love with him.*

He grabs his phone so angrily, his blood boiling to the surface as he gets ready to call Kez.

He starts to tap the number as a million spiteful and malicious thoughts flash through his brain as he prepares to let him have it. He stops halfway through pressing the digits and let's the phone fall from his hand onto the bed sheets. His anger, instantly dissipated, when he sees the picture on his screen saver of his phone of him, Kez and Maria the night of the karaoke.

He takes a few minutes, looking at the way Kez was holding him. He sees the way his body was completely shrouded in Kez's hands and arms. Holding him so lovingly, his embrace, un diminishing. The look on his face full of adoration for him.

This couldn't be the face of someone who would so ruthlessly cheat, could it?!

A similar dizziness to the drunken state he was in the previous night, takes hold of him.

He bites his lip hard and sniffs back his tears. He opens another door to the chaise longue on the other side of the bed and takes a T shirt of Kez's and puts it on. *I am NOT going to let this bastard determine the outcome of my day! I need to pull myself together and get to the studio. Talk about fuel to feed the fire. At this rate I will be singing with so much raw emotion, that anyone else in the room might question if it's appropriate to be listening to such levels of pain and hurt.*

He takes a piece of paper from the side table and scribbles in big letters.

' *How could you?* Don't ever call me again!!! '

Making sure that all the wardrobe doors are visibly open, clearly confirming the reason for the chastising note, he opens the door and leaves the the building for the last time.

Theo silently thanks the weather for being cold enough that his tearful watering eyes do not seem out of place as the icy blasts of wind hit his face with full force. He walks with purpose and with enough strength to get him to the underground for the short tube journey to the studio.

A few minutes pass by and the platform starts to fill up with people, desperate to get to work, arriving minutes before the train is due to arrive. At the end of the platform, next to Theo, what can only be described as a lovers tiff, breaks out. Broken sentences here and there could be heard above the announcer stating that there will be a delay of five minutes.

" That's the problem with you, you just don't fucking listen! " She says.

He retaliates with. " You're wrong! I do listen, it's just that what comes out of your stupid mouth makes no fucking sense.. at all!! "

The endless back and forth between the two, mixed with the triviality of the reason for the argument makes something inside Theo snap. He turns and looks at the couple, listening before saying.

" Guys, can you keep it down please. I'm having a *really really* bad day. I'd genuinely appreciate it if you could wait until you get home to continue ragging at each other. "

The man, furiously staring back at Theo shouts. " Shut up man! This is none of your business! "

" Okay, fine, I'm shutting up. " He says shaking his head.

The man, unable to let it go, continues. " No seriously, why do you think this is any of your business? "

" How long have you been together? " Theo says, blindsiding him.

" What? " The man says stepping towards Theo, his girlfriend in tow.

" It's a simple question..How long? Two years, three? "

The couple look at Theo, perplexed by his increasing intervention.

" Well? " He says calmly waiting for the two to answer.

" Five actually, why? "

" Happy? "

"For the most part, yes. " His girlfriend answers as her boyfriend interjects.

" What the hell does all this mean to you? "

" *Nothing*. Your relationship doesn't mean anything to me, at all. " He says, suddenly aware that everyone on the platform has, unusually for Londoners, directed their attention towards the three of them." Does it mean anything to you? Because believe me, from where I'm standing, it doesn't sound like either of you appreciate what you have. "

" Listen mate, you don't understand what it's like to have her nagging every time I do something wrong. "

" No I don't. I don't know what it's like, but let me ask you this. Has he cheated on you? "

" No, but.."

" How about her, has she cheated on you? "

" No, but that's not the point though.. I- "

" Well, let me tell you this. I *do* know what it's like to be cheated on. *That* to me, is a *damn* good reason to be angry with your partner at eight o clock in the morning. *Not* what you are both arguing about whilst I, and everyone else here on the platform, have to listen to and endure. "

" All very well for you to say that, you're probably single! "

" Well, I wasn't until about thirty minutes ago, but do you see me letting rip on my phone even though I've not long found out that my second boyfriend in a row has cheated on me with a woman in the space of one week? "

" Well, you're obviously doing something wrong in the bedroom, mate. Maybe I should let you talk to my girlfriend for a bit. At least she knows how to suck dick. " He says turning and walking away.

Without thinking Theo says under his breath. " I very much doubt that since there clearly isn't anything there to suck in the first place. "

Hearing this, the man flies at Theo. Just as his fist is about to make contact with his face, Theo is eclipsed by a tall, muscular man who grabs the man's hand and pushes him back, away from them. The man, not turning, says in a familiar bass filled voice. " T, are you ok there? I ran over as soon as I recognised your voice. "

" Darryl? Is that you? "

" The very same." He says watching the man, who, looking undeterred, shouts something incoherently as the approaching train drowns out his voice.

" Yeah yeah! Pipe down princess! Keep it moving. " Says Darryl.

Seeing the man disappear onto the train, Darryl turns and faces Theo. He smiles to reveal the whitest teeth with two gold teeth shining brightly on the upper left hand side.

" I'm glad I was here at the right place at the right time. " He says taking off his aviator glasses, " Otherwise, that could have ended in a very different way, and I don't think our budget would have stretched to your rhinoplasty. "

Theo smiles briefly before his voice starts to crack and he starts to cry. " It's just been a really tough first couple of hours, just ignore me. "

Darryl instinctively holds on to him. " I heard...I'm really sorry to hear that though, man. "

Theo shakes his head and exhales, his breath shaky, before looking up at him. " Not the best impression on my first day at work, is it? " He says drying his eyes. " I'm sorry for leaking all over you. "

He taps Theo on the back. " S'all good lil one, just concentrate on channeling all that hatred and anger into the studio when we get there.. "

" Oh, I will, you don't have to worry about that. " He says attempting to dry his eyes as they continue to produce more tears, involuntarily.

He pulls out what looks like a white gold hip flask. " You want a stiff one? "

Theo laughs, then attempts to cover it up with a cough.

" Always. "

" Here, take a sip. That'll soon dry you up. This is our train, hop on T. " He says as the bullet of speed slows until it comes to a grinding halt.

They take the last two seats in the front carriage, as people continue to fill up the carriages and mill in between the people sat down whilst holding on to the blue bars protruding from the ceiling to the floor.

Theo boldly speaks above the ever solemn travelling general public. " I have to admit, I didn't expect to see you on a common tube station. Aren't you music big wig types normally chauffeured everywhere. Or am I wrong? "

" I like the train, I like to keep it real. Keeps me grounded, reminds me of growing up in New York. "

Theo smiles to himself, as the gentle giant continues to talk. He can't help but think to himself how funny it is that he talks like a stereotypical New Yorker. Not in a bad way, quite the opposite in fact. It was unexpectedly comforting that he sounds identical to the guys on the television shows he grew up watching with his mum. He sits quietly and listens to every word that he says, finding him to be strangely hypnotic with his dulcet tones.

" Don't you think T? " He says tapping his foot to rhythm of the train passing through another station.

" I'm so sorry, I have to admit I didn't hear a word of what you said after I asked the question. I was just listening to your accent and then that's all I was hearing. Of course, now I'm embarrassed because I must seem like such a disinterested asshole. "

" Don't sweat it T, you good by me. " He says patting his shoulder. " I was saying that I like the sound of the train on the tracks. It gets my mind fresh with ideas for beats, rhythms and all that. "

" Mine's when I'm the shower and the doors don't quite close so they knock back and forth sounding like a bass drum. "

Darryl smiles and nods in agreement. " See, that's what I'm talkin' about man, you got grooves going through you. It's in your veins. "

The train starts to slow, indicating that it's time to get off again.The two disembark at the Tottenham Court Road stop to avoid the manic people traffic at Leicester Square. They make their way out of the station, and head towards Dean Street, via Shaftesbury Avenue where the cold air greets them once again.

" I have to admit I haven't heard that accent before since I've been here, where you from son? " He says strutting down the street, his hand under his chin stroking his neatly kept five o clock shadow.

" Somerset, but my accent is a mish mash of the south west and other places. My parents were always moving around. We moved so much that sometimes I'd wake up and check outside my window to make sure I recognised the same streets. " He watches how Darryl seems enthralled by his dialect. " Growing up, I never had friends, I barely had a fri- let alone an - end. " He says.

" The accent.. It's cute, real cute. " He says waiting to hear the next thing Theo says.

" I can recite the stops on the jubilee line if it does it that much for you. " He says jokingly.

Daryl's face changes instantly from it's smiling hypnotic state to serious brooding face. " My bad T, didn't mean to make you uncomfortable and all that. "

" You didn't. Genuinely, you didn't! " He says warmly smiling at him. " It's just my sense of humour, I'm a little sharp sometimes, probably sharper than usual after this morning but please don't take me the wrong way.. I'm a nice guy really.. Unless I'm in front of trash like a few minutes ago. "

" I know, what's the deal with that? I thought New Yorkers could be rude! " He says playing with his diamond earrings. " He's lucky he stepped away though, I'm from the Bronx so he wouldn't have stood a chance against me. He would have been under that train quicker than He could spell it. "

" So, how long have you been writing music for? " Theo quizzes.

" Since I was a baby. "

" Now come on Darryl, that's a bit over the top. You can't tell me you were sat in the womb scratching notes out on her inner wall. "

Darryl winces. " Well, maybe not from birth, but close. I will say this much though. I must have had some obsession with chords whilst in the womb, since I'd wrapped the umbilical one around my neck during labour. "

" Ouch! Your poor mum, that must have been traumatic! "

" Yesir! Apparently, I nearly died."

" Perhaps I should go down to the local maternity ward and grab one of those to use on Kez. "

Darryl just looks at him, no words necessary.

" No, I know, and I promise I won't go on about it, but what's with guys? Why do they find it so easy to lie?

Are they taken aside at school and given special classes on how to be a prize cunt? "

" I can just see it now, a group of young boys with different timetables to the girls. " Darryl laughs.

" First period Polygamy, followed by second period Physical Degradation, and every other period is a free one, because that's how they learn how to be lazy as fuck! " He spouts emphatically as another man, walking towards them, smiles in the direction of a Theo, almost as if in agreement.

Darryl looks over at Theo, smiling awkwardly as they walk steadily.

Theo, realising that he has become quite hot tempered, covers his face completely with his hands. " Oh shit, I'm sorry, I'm making you feel uncomfortable. That's the last thing I want to do. Especially since you were so gallant stepping in to come to my rescue. "

" Not at all Theo, it just sucks for you is all. you guys looked pretty tight last night. Just didn't have him pegged as the cheating type. "

" Me either, but it seems like I'm following a pattern here. So I think the best thing I can do for now, is exactly what I'm going to be doing today, which is throwing myself back into music. "

" Amen to that brother. " He says reopening his hip flask again and taking another swig, before passing to Theo.

" So, who's your musical influences T? I definitely hear some Stevie and some Marvin in your voice, and your falsetto rings of the modern artists like Maxwell. " They pause for a bit, Darryl scanning Theo's face for clues. " Now hear me out on the next one, because you might not know them, but I get this crazy feel that you sing with her influences. "

" I'm intrigued. " Theo says, crossing one leg in front of the other, whilst doing the same with both arms. " Go ahead. "

" Well, I don't know if she was popular over here, but her name is Amel Larrieux. "

" FUCK OFF! " He bolts back upright as some passers by, shift nervously at his outburst. " You did not just mention one of my all time favourite singers?! "

In almost an instant, Theo forgets all the negative things happening in his life, and instead, feels genuinely enthralled that a fellow human being can relate to her beautiful, soulful, yet vulnerable vocal talents.

Darryl, for the first time, changes his stance from laid back strutting, to unending enthusiasm. He slows his pace as they approach the studio located opposite the French House pub. The building, an unmistakably classy strip of black from top to bottom. The signage of the studio, situated to the top right in silver, and below, the jet black doors with gold knobs command attention.

" What? No way! I was right, you know my home girl?
" He says pushing the door open and leading the way
through to a large studio. The red room, divided into
borders by a thick horizontal strip of white running
through the centre of each wall, is filled with an array
of instruments from electric guitars to a grand piano.
The impressive night sky of blue lights giving the
appearance of being somewhere between a
planetarium and the royal variety performance, whilst
the homeliness of the wooden polished floor, creates
an open space.

Theo takes a breath in awe of the beautiful
surroundings, feeling that it would not be unrealistic
to pinch himself hard to convince himself he was
there. Darryl gives him a few moments to absorb the
atmosphere before continuing.

" I remember the first time she sang, ' Half that makes
me Whole ' in my studio back in Brooklyn. I was so
moved, so touched, so honoured she graced those
four walls with her sensual tones. She completely
blew me away.. and that's the vibe I got from you
when I saw you that night. Your energy and your vibe,
it was just off the chain, T. "

" Thank you so much for believing in me, let's just
hope I can do you justice. Right where do you want
me. "

For the next few hours the two guys worked through
song after song. Theo's heartfelt, honest lyrical

approach to story telling coupled with Darryl's unique beats and epic production, meant that there was no end to their creative flow. Theo loved every second of being back. For the first time in ages he could easily forget the men who had affected his life for the past few years. He could breathe and his inner voice could finally do the talking again.

" Right, we need to wrap this up for today T, I've got an appointment I gotta get to, but you free for tomorrow? We can pick up where we left off? " Darryl says into the microphone in the mixing room.

" Definitely. " Theo says beaming from ear to ear, mesmerised by the aforementioned stars until Darryl joins him in the room again. " I want to thank you so much for today, I really needed this. I think..no, *I know* that I'd lost a lot of myself in my search for love and romance. Plus, I feel like I've exorcised some series relationship demons today! " He says laughing.

" My pleasure T, all my pleasure. " Darryl says warmly, standing next to him.

" Okay, I'll see you tomorrow mister New York. Say about eight o clock again? " Theo says stepping away from the microphone and removing his headphones. He starts to walks in front of Darryl, just past eye level, when suddenly he is pulled back by his arm until he is right in front of him again.

" Are you okay? Is everything alright? " Theo says casually.

Darryl, silently looks Theo up and down, before whispering nervously. " It will be when I've done this. " Then, without warning, before Theo has time to think, he places his lips fully over Theo's and kisses him hard and aggressively. To his surprise, and delight, Theo doesn't appear to resist. Instead, Theo yields into his arms and kisses him back. " I wanted you from the second I saw you up on stage singing T, you're so hot! Then, when I saw you last night.. I was like, damn! I need to get wit' him. "

Theo, as if a bubble bursting, or a spell breaking, he jolts his head away. Confused, yet undeniably aroused, he pulls himself away from him. " I..I.. need to go.. I mean... you need to go.. I need to get myself sex.. I mean *set* for tonight with Maria... Umm.. see you tomorrow morning? we can pick up where we left off."

" Hell yeah we can." Darryl drawls.

" No, I didn't mean, you know what I mean.. You get me? "

" I do Theo," He says licking his lips as Theo hastily disappears from sight, " and *you* will too, tomorrow. "

" Kez has done *what?!* " Maria says sipping her Soho Porn Star Martini as she listens to the events of Theo's day, at an ever crowded yet fun natured, bar Soho. She stands in shock, leaning on the spotless chrome bar, the flickering imagery of cartoons on the nineteen forties retro television sets above, mocking the slapstick nature of his revelations.

" Then *you* did what? Oh my god Theo! I really don't know what the fuck is going on anymore. *I can't keep up with*
you! "

He momentarily perches himself on a hexagonal bar stool, and locks his feet under the buckled grey frame.

" What else was I supposed to do? The evidence was irrefutable.. Women's clothing, yet he lives alone. Pictures all over the house, that I might add, were never there when we first fucked. " He rambles, only stopping to let Maria speak.

She points towards the abstract yet cohesive ceiling, filled with quotes and funky imagery of famous people and highlights one in particular that reads :

Knowledge Speaks But Wisdom Listens.

" All I'm saying is, can you really be sure though T? I mean I'm pretty sure that when you were there, the last thing on your mind would have been how he'd arranged his bedroom decor whilst his cock was rammed down your throat? "

" Honestly Maria, I know what I *didn't* see last time.. There was definitely no pictures. Admittedly, as for the clothes I wouldn't have had a clue, because I never went near his wardrobe. "

" Well, you wouldn't would you? The idea of opening one of those puppies would probably break you out in a sweat! After all, you're far from a closet case! "

" Exactly! No fucking Narnia for me! I'll leave that to the sad ass men I seem to keep choosing! " He knocks back one of the seven deadly sins cocktails before indicating to Maria for them to move to the merry-go-round themed section opposite, to the previously occupied yellow cart.

" Honey, I'm not defending Kez, because I don't know for definite.. but are you sure you want to throw it all away? I just don't *buy* that he's *bi*?! " She says nearly forgetting to collect their remaining Lust, and Greed. " He just looked *so* into you last night, and I mean movie style into you. "

" That's what I thought, but.." He waits for a second, stroking the fairground horse, before speaking. " Look, I'm open to suggestions, but you need to just give me a plausible reason for why he has women's clothes in the wardrobe.. Oh and also kids clothes too. I forgot to mention that! "

" I don't know! I honestly don't know..but then what the fuck do I know? I mean, if you'd told me that Chris would have thrown me under the bus and then backed up over me until I'm roadkill, I would have said ' no way! ' but it didn't stop it happening. "

Theo taps her lightly on the top of her hand. " I know sis, I know.. this dating stuff.. Is it just me, or is it toxic? How on earth are you supposed to make foundations when all you have to work with is the fakery of foundation itself? "

" I know, it's awful." She thinks for a minute. " If it helps, I spent last night with the man who I've had a crush on for months, only to end up with a cum stain on a four thousand pound outfit, and an apology. " She says looking back at the wall of glass, peppered with yellow carousel lights, bordered by wooden squares.

" Excuse me?! Why am I only hearing this now? You left that part out! " He says staring intensely into her eyes." Come on, tell all! "

She leans in, meeting his gaze. " Okay, so we get back to his place and things are great. He starts to get undressed, and let me tell you this... Who'd have thought the power suits he wore, day in, day out, would have been hiding such a beautiful, glistening, muscular body."

" Seriously Hun, you need to stop it, you're turning me on! " He says realising that his hand is still stroking the horses mane.

" Oh really? That's something I'd definitely be interested in seeing." A random man says squeezing by.

" Keep moving mister, not going to happen! " He says without acknowledging him. " So, beautiful naked body, what happens next? "

" Well, he starts to kiss me.. Which was very promising because he was an *exceptionally* good kisser. "

" Great, always important. " Theo continues to listen whilst taking a sip of his Greed.

She continues. " We rub up next to each other, I'm grinding against his dick and he's rock hard. So I reach down to touch him and my hand is met with wet. "

" Precum? No? " Theo says.

" I wish! No, he had definitely heat his meat! " She says waving her hand in the air, narrowly missing the waiter walking by.

" How embarrassing for him! What did he do next? "

" He just kept apologising and then made about ten excuses of things he needed to get back to. "

" At eleven o clock at night, like one does. " Theo says sarcastically.

" Right.. Then he left without another word, and I haven't had a text, or a phone call.. Not a sausage. "

" Clearly you didn't get a sausage. Otherwise we would be having a very different kind of conversation right about now. "

Maria sighs and rests her head on his shoulder. " I'm feeling kind of blah, do you want to get a takeaway, it's only seven thirty. We can rent a movie and go back to mine? "

" Sounds like a plan. What with all the talk of sausages, I'm starting to feel like a piece of meat sat around here. " As yet another man leers over Theo.

After leaving uncharacteristically early, they head towards Yoshino, a Japanese delicatessen on Shaftesbury Avenue. Maria gets her usual Chicken Katsu Curry and Theo gets a portion of Vegetable Tempura Rolls and a container of Miso soup. They walk and talk, casually enjoying the neighbourhood that had become so familiar to them both from the many nights they had spent at Maria's. Theo could always recognise how close they were to her place by the familiar landmarks. The big oak tree set back from the road, the surprisingly graffiti free telephone box, and the man sprawled out on his front on Maria's doorstep..

" Maria! Who's that? " Theo says, slightly concerned. " Do you know who that is? "

" I don't, but he has definitely had a skinful. " She says laughing.

Theo approaches the man. " Maria, I didn't think he's drunk, he's barely moving."

He leans in closer.

" *Maria call an ambulance, he's not breathing!* " He says hurriedly checking his pulse. He starts to move the stranger into a position where he can attempt resuscitation and recoils when he realises who it is.

Maria, whilst holding the phone waiting for it to connect, sees him react so severely. " *What is it T?? What's*
wrong?? "
" It's Leon, I think he's taken an overdose!!! "

CHAPTER 12

" Clear! " The paramedic shouts, the paddles charged and ready to tempt Leon back from his fading existence.

" Hun it's going to be okay. He said that it was good that we got here early. " Theo says comforting the crumpled mess on the floor that is Maria.

Unable to answer him through streaming eyes, she squeezes his hand tightly whilst the other one holds the inevitable suicide note.

Theo turns and scowls at some of the people who have gathered around. They were looking over Maria's shoulder, whispering and judging her, after seeing the note. " I think you've all gawped enough, don't you? If you must know, this woman in front of you, used to be in love this man. *So give her that much respect whilst she fights with him!* "

The crowd disperse slowly, looking sheepish, until it is just the two best friends, her former partner and the three paramedics left.

As the man working on Leon continues to shock him, he suddenly stops and reaches for his wrist.

" We have a pulse! Bag him and let's get going! " The guy says purposefully looking over at Theo and Maria.

" Come on you two, we're going to take him to the University College A & E on Euston Road. Normally it would be family only, but since we can't make contact and he needs familiar voices around him, there's space in the ambulance for you both. "

Theo thanks the man and helps Maria into the ambulance and onto the seat next to Leon's stretcher all the while holding his hand.

" Maria, it's not your fault. " Theo says looking into her eyes, knowing her well enough to know the thoughts that would be racing through her head.

" He clearly thinks so. " She says, taking disjointed breaths and handing him the note.

Theo reads the tear stained note:

   " Dear Maria,

                If you are reading this letter then I have succeeded in saying goodbye to this world. I hope you can find it in your heart to know that I just can't go on any longer. The pain I feel can't go on any more. I know I should have talked to you sooner after we lost the baby, but I can't help but blame myself for the loss of our child. I know you have told me that it wasn't my fault, but *how* could you believe that it wasn't?

I find myself waking up every morning, and for a brief second, I look over expecting to see you laying there. Our beautiful boy would come bounding in to the room, begging for our attention. Wide eyed and excited at the new experiences that would be coming his way. Yet as I lay there, the stark reality jolts me back into this un ending pain. All I have left to see, are the cold walls and the empty space where you should be. Still loving me, still happy to be mine..

You once said, " If you love something , you have to set it free and if it comes back to you, then it's yours. If it doesn't then it was never yours in the first place. " Well, that night you did come back to me. That night you were in my arms, and I allowed myself to believe that I was finally getting you back. That morning, I woke to see that you had gone, and my renewed existence had instantly turned back into the familiar living nightmare that I had dreaded for the past six months.

I'm sorry that I have burdened you with my pain, and I'm sorry that I could not be enough for you to try again. I can only assume that the other night, when we made love again, it must have brought back too many painful memories and that a reconciliation was completely out of the question.

Since we first parted, I have tried to rebuild my life, and I had been on a few dates. Nothing serious. Yet I have not been able to find someone as warm, special, and kind as you my sweet. So, forgive me and try to understand, I cannot do this life alone anymore.

Now, and always.
All my love
Leon.

" Oh Maria! You can't take what he says in this note so literally? If a person has made up their mind to end their life, it is never the responsibility or fault of any exterior person or influence. You didn't make him neck that bottle of painkillers. "

" Listen to your friend. He's right you know. " The paramedic says checking Leon's vitals.

" I know logically, it's not my fault.. but I should never have drunkenly gone back home with him that night. "

" Why? Because if you hadn't, he would have been only *slightly* suicidal? Is that what you think? " He says in bad taste.

" No, but at least I wouldn't have felt connected to the reason that pushed him over the edge to do this."

He crouches down in front to face her. " Hun, he was miserable before any of this happened. You did actually *read* the note properly? No? I can understand if you hadn't, what with all the liquid seeping from every orifice on your face dripping onto the note. "

She starts to laugh through the tears. " You've always been so inappropriate at the wrong times.. but I love you for it Theo. "

The paramedic, Femi, smiles to himself, understanding Theo's attempt at humour to lighten the mood.

Leon's hand suddenly squeezes Maria's.

" He's starting to come around guys..." He maintains eye contact with the patient. " It's okay Leon, you're okay, we're on our way to the hospital. Just try to relax. "

He murmurs something inaudible and looks in the direction of Maria, trying to pull his ventilator off. Theo seeing this reaffixes the mask.

" Ah ah ah," he says, " don't you think you've tried hard enough to kill yourself for one day.. Let go of the mask, that's a good boy. " He says smiling.

" You're really funny, man. " Femi says," Are you single? Because I think my brother would lap you up. "

" Lap me up? Why? Is he a Dachshund? " Theo says with wit." Thanks for the offer, but I think I've had enough dogs to last me a lifetime. "

" Stop it man, you're killing me. " He pleads whilst trying to stifle laughter. " Seriously, he's really handsome and intelligent, and he has a great job. "

Theo looks over at Maria trying not to laugh. " Wow! I thought me and my brother were close, but you're taking it to a whole other level.. Are you sure *you* don't want to date him? "

Maria cuts in." He's definitely got enough on his plate Femi.. How about you? Do you have much on *your* plate, cos if not, I can fix that. "

He smiles at her, blushing through his handsome face.

" Maria, you know how you were saying *I* was inappropriate... " He says pointing discreetly and whispers as best as he can in the cramped ambulance. " *Take a look around you before you say anymore.* "

" Huh? " She responds, oblivious.

He continues to point and whisper. *"We've only just got him back, let's not try and send him over the edge just yet! "*

" Oh fuck! " She says, realising what Theo was referring to before attempting to backtrack on herself.

" Oh, you thought I was talking for me? No! My friend.. Jenny, you remember Jenny? "

" Of course! Jenny.. from the block! Got you. " Theo says mocking her.

She shoots him a glare.

Femi, picking up on the awkwardness, rescues her. " I'm flattered, but I'm married. "

" Oh, really? So where's the wedding ring? " She says instinctually without thinking what he was trying to do. " *I mean, good for you! that's great!* "

" Are we nearly there yet? " Theo says exasperated.

" Shouldn't be too much longer Theo." He says, setting up the drip. " Now before we get to the hospital, and I have to disappear to my next callout ... Are you sure you don't want me to give you my brothers number? "

Looking over at Maria, unsure of his decision, Theo starts to speak before she answers for him." Oh! Go

on Theo, take his number, what have you got to lose?"
Maria says nudging him.

" My dignity, my confidence, my general positive outlook, my faith in men.. Do you want me to continue? " He says.

" Theo, I promise you, he's a good man. Plus, he's actually my half brother. His mother is Spanish. So he's not just a hot guy, he's a hot Blatino guy! "

" Watch your fingers Femi! He'll bite them right off! " She says, watching Theo's eyes widen in interest.

" Alright Davina, this isn't Street Mate! " He says taking the number from the paramedic. " You are right though, you smug bitch. I would have to be a fool to turn that offer down. Thank you Femi. What, may I ask is his name? "

" It's Marcellino. "

" Ooh Theo and Marcellino, sitting in a *tree*, f u c k I n g. " Maria says imitating the school rhyme.

" I hardly think that's the kind of wood I'd want to be experiencing sis. "

" Do you have a picture of him? Let me see if this man is good enough for my T. " Maria says ignoring her best friend.

As Femi pulls out his phone and locates a few pictures, the three of them gather around near Leon's head.

" I never thought I would see the day I would be glad that someone we knew would try to top themselves. "

Theo says practically drooling over Marcellino. " He's a model, no? "

" Unsurprisingly, he has done some before. " The proud brother boasts.

" So, you and I will be brothers in law, huh? " Theo says smiling and nudging him. " I guess it's a good thing that you like me already isn't it? "

" You joke about it, but I know my brothers taste, and he will be happy as a pig in shit when he meets you. "

" Nice...I think. " He says, giving back the phone.

The ambulance pulls up to the front of the hospital and two eager nurses greet them at the entrance to take Leon into the building. Relieved and secure in the knowledge that Leon's status has drastically improved, Maria and Theo take a seat outside the now closed canteen. Theo rummages around in his coat pocket to get some change for the drinks vending machine.

" We certainly know how to make it an eventful night, no? "

" That we do Theo, that we do. " She says taking the overly full cappuccino.

He takes his Mocha and joins her on the plastic seats. " You got a near dead ex and I'll be getting some rampant sex."

" Yeah.. About that, what are you going to do? "

He looks at her in surprise. " What do you mean? Do you want me to go into details about what I'm going to be doing sexually with Marcellicious? "

" No, I mean, technically you are still seeing Kez, aren't you? I mean he knows you're mad with him, but you guys haven't officially broken up? "

" Well, technically you are still seeing Reuben, aren't you? I mean does he know he's fucked it up? " He says imitating her with the exact same voice.

" He's been texting me throughout the journey here, I just didn't see them until now. " She says exhaling heavily.

"Oh, has he now? What's he been saying? "

" The usual stuff guys say when they lose self discipline. ' This has never happened to me before ' and, ' it's only cos I'm so attracted to you' and my favourite ' let me make it up to you, it won't happen again. ' "

" Well, they are probably all true statements. " Theo rationalises, taking a sip of the piping hot drink.

" Well, quite frankly, I don't want to take a chance on him violating any more of my favourite clothes. " She says sharply.

" Maria! Come on! You know your crush is bound to be feeling so awful about the accident. Is this really a fair cum-uppance. " He says with innuendo.. " You should definitely give him another chance. Just tell him to knock one out before he comes over next time. "

" I don't know, I'll think on it.. "

A commotion at the end of the hallway entrance stops Maria's sentence. They both look over and see the back of a man stumbling through the corridor, his leg limping slightly, holding onto his bunched up hand.

" Ouch, that looks pretty awful! did you see the blood? " Maria winces in empathy.

" I did. " He shakes his head.

She looks around the canteen and reminisces. " You know what, I actually applied for a job in a hospital a few days ago, but once it came around to the interview date, I just couldn't do it. I never realised it, until then, but I hate these places. They make me feel so uncomfortable. "

Theo nods in agreement before suddenly remembering.

" Oh, talking of interviews.. you never did tell me how the interview went? "

" Well, you never told me that your school year reunion was tomorrow night either, but you don't hear me complaining." She says, blindsiding Theo.

Theo, looking genuinely surprised and flabbergasted at her knowledge of this, slowly speaks. " *How the hell did you know about that* ! I threw that invitation away the second it came through the door! "

" Well, you know the catering job.." She starts.

He takes a few confused moments before realising what she was indicating. " *No way! Thats just creepy!*

You're telling me, that of all the catering jobs you could have been lined up for, it ends up being.."

She nods in agreement of the unbelievable coincidence.

" I know! " She smiles shaking her head, still amazed at the turn of events. " It still doesn't explain why *you're* not going though. " She says knowing full well the reason.

" I don't know, I just don't feel like it. I've outgrown them and I don't really care to touch base or anything for that matter. "

" You're missing the point of a school reunion Hun! Its more about gloating at how much better your life is than the alcoholic, sex deprived, career failing existences your class mates are probably now leading. "

They both look at each other stonily at the irony.

" So moving on, swiftly. " She says. " I'm not stupid Theo, I do know the real reason, but just as a drug addict has to confess the words out loud in a rehab centre, I'm begging you to tell me the reason. "

" Yes, Kieran is part of the reason. "

She looks at him questioningly.

"*Alright! alright! it's the whole reason!* "

She puts out her hand and grabs his and rubs it.

" Seriously Maria, you know what happened to me! In graphic detail, I might add. That man was nearly the death of me! You cant seriously blame me.. I just think that if I ever saw his fucking face again, I'm pretty sure I'd actually rip it from his skull, literally! "

" I do know that Theo, believe me there are parts of *me* that would love to poison his food with arsenic, or at least give him a bad case of diarrhoea, but it isn't going to change anything. Wouldn't you love to be able to go in there and look him in the face and tell him that he *didn't* break you? "

He looks at her, knowing that she's right, and rolls his eyes.

" Plus, you get to tell everyone that you're going to be a worldwide recording star! I bet none of them can profess to anything as spectacular as that! " She smiles warmly.

A doctor, wearing what appears to be a vomit stained white coat, walks into the canteen and straight up to them." Maria Martinez and Theo Morrison? "

They both nod.

" Leon is stable and he's asking to see you. " He says informing Maria.

Maria, looking helpless, looks back at the doctor. " I don't think.. I can't.. It's just that.. "

Theo interrupts her, sensing the difficulty in her voice. " If it's okay, I'll take this one doctor... He knows me too, and I don't think either one of them would benefit from seeing each other at this moment in time, no matter how much he thinks they will. "

The doctor looks at Maria for a moment, before acknowledging him. " Okay, I trust that you know better than I do as to why it wouldn't be a good idea. Are you sure that you don't want to see him Miss Martinez? "

She nods briefly before turning, looks warmly at Theo and mouths ' thank you ' as he disappears with him.

" Stupid question, but how are you feeling? " Theo asks as he sits down next to a disappointed looking Leon.

" Well, considering I've had enough charcoal shoved down my throat to fuel ten barbecues and more tubes going through me than the london underground. I'm doing okay. " He replies quietly.

" Well, that is what happens when you swallow a whole bottle of pills at once. You do know they're not smarties? " He says offering him some ice chips.

" You got me there. " He splutters and coughs trying not to laugh. " Is Maria coming to see me? " He says hopefully.

Theo looks away towards the corridor before turning back and looking him in the eyes. " Im afraid not Leon, she.. " He thinks carefully how to word it. " She wants to, but she doesn't want to make the situation worse than it already is. "

" In what way does she think it will be worse?! " He splutters whilst gesturing to the drips coming out of his arms. " I knew it, she does blame me.. I secretly hoped that she didn't, but she can't bear to be around me, can she? "

Theo squeezes his shoulder reassuringly. " No you misunderstand, its not that she hates you, or holds any kind of blame towards you. She knows as well as anyone does, that there is *nothing* to blame. "

" Of course there is! " He says, thinking before speaking again. " I... I... I made it happen, I *know* I did. "

Theo leans in before blurting out. *" Leon you can't fuck a baby to death by having sex with your pregnant girlfriend!* There has *never* been a recorded case in the world of *any* woman miscarrying for that reason. "

Leon, genuinely surprised, stutters. " What? I assumed.. the next morning.. he was gone.."

Theo continues calmly. " You neither indirectly, or directly killed your child. Its just one of the many sad, unexplainable things that will happen to a human being in our lifetime.. you need to understand this Leon. Its not your fault. "

He puts his hand to his face." So, if that's the case.. Why can't she love me? What did I do wrong? " He says half confused, and half struggling not to break down into tears. " Why cant we start again.. I miss her Theo, I miss her so much.. Sometimes, when I think about her and how good it was, I genuinely forget how to breathe. "

Theo, instead of answering with a positive, back slapping comment to make him feel better, just smiles sympathetically. After all, no one could relate to loss more than Theo could right now. It was less than a day ago that the second painful blow to Theo's heart had firmly planted itself deeply in him. Every time he thinks about the perfect man he thought he had found, the knight in shining armour that had been so ever presently there for him, his soul yearned a little more. He still couldn't quite understand how he had not seen it.

Surely after experiencing bisexuality so up close and personal, you would think I would be the last person to be caught out by it again. The man who held me so passionately in the moonlight, the tears of joy welling up in his eyes as he looked deep into My eyes. It just didn't make sense..

" You know what Leon, you just have to take one day at a time... And never forget to breathe.." He takes a few moments to understand how to put it into words. " I can't pretend that the pain will ever go away.. You *will* think less and less about it until eventually it will just feel more like a dull pain instead of the fresh stabbing you feel right now. " He waits, looking at Leon to see if his words settle. " It's not all bad though.. At least you'll get some pretty good sleep tonight with all those drugs coursing through your veins. "

He smiles, a single tear making it's way down his pale face.

" I have to admit.. One thing is clear. "

" What's that? "

" Being that close to death and seeing everything fade away.. I realised that even though I feel like I'm in hell, it is *nothing* compared to an afterlife of feeling nothing but a world of ' what if's ' " He turns over to face away from Theo.

As Theo turns to walk out of the hospital room, he hears Leon say. " Thanks for caring Theo. You are a lovely guy and I really appreciate you popping by. Take care of her for me. "

On rejoining Maria in the hallway, Theo grabs another drink, this time a decaffeinated coffee. He looks at her with a turned down, half hearted smile.

" How was he? " She cautiously asks. " Forget that. That's a dumb thing to ask. Of course I know how he is.. I was with him for long enough to know how his heart is feeling right now. "

" He's old enough to take care of himself Hun. "

" Yeah, looked like it earlier tonight when he was foaming at the mouth. " She says quickly.

" He will be fine now. Now he knows the truth. It's just a matter of time until he works through all the misplaced guilt he has carried around for months. "

Maria looks over Theo's shoulder and loses concentration.

" Hey Theo, that guy with the limp, from earlier.. Isn't that him in the distance coming towards us? I know we never saw his face the first time, and we can't see it now, but he's limping the same way. I wonder what happened to him? "

" I think you're right. " Theo takes a glance over in his direction, not taking much notice of him, still thinking about Leon. " He's probably some drunken idiot thinking he can solve his problems with his fists instead of talking things through. "

" Oh, those types. " Maria says. " The ones that can't even say the word syllable, let alone understand what it means. "

" Exactly! Evidently the men I attract seem to be struggling with the same thing about the word monogamy! "

Maria laughs lightly, distracted again by the approaching man. This time she nudges Theo. " *Hun, is that who I think it is?* "

As the man edges closer, the familiarity of his features become more apparent with every step. The man is wearing the same clothes as Kez. He has the same body frame and height as Kez. It is only when he lifts his head, that the two can see that it is in fact, Kez.

" I'm *definitely* not ready for this Maria! Let's get the fuck out of here! I have no interest in hearing anything come out of his lying, two timing, woman fucking, albeit beautiful, mouth of his. " Theo shouts, deliberately in ear shot of Kez.

Kez, recognising Theo's voice, with new energy, leaps into action. " *Theo!! It's not what you..* "

Kez tries to grab Theo's arm, but fails to make contact as he aggressively pulls away. " If you finish that sentence, trust me I will *break* that *other* hand! "

" If you just let me speak for one minute T! Can't you give me that at least?? You *really* have got it completely

twisted. "

" Oh this I really want to hear.. Don't tell me, the clothes in the wardrobe just happened to be laying around perfectly arranged in order of skirts, dresses, work suits?.."

" It can all be explained T, come on it's.. " He says weakly, trying to attach himself to him.

Theo interrupts, unrelenting. " Oh and the pictures in every room, at every turn, of *you* and *her*.. " He takes a breath before recalling. " And *YOUR CHILD APPARENTLY!!! I mean FUCK ME how did you think you were gonna keep that a secret?!* "

" LISTEN THEO! " Kez says, finally grabbing his face firmly, inadvertently smudging him with blood. " They *are* my family, but they're *not* my wife and kid! They neede.. "

The presence of a woman in surgical scrubs stops Theo and Kez in their tracks.

" I was wondering where you had got to. I just wanted you to know that we have cleaned up your sister. Luckily, she hasn't sustained much injury. There are a few sprains from when she must have fallen trying to escape him, and a couple of bruises from when he first hit her on entering the property. Nothing too serious, but she's understandably shaken and traumatised. I'm just thankful that you were able to reach her before... Well, let's just say, I see a lot of domestic abuse in this job on a day to day basis, and it doesn't always end this well. You got to her just in time before anything really nasty happened. " She looks down at his bloodied hand. " I have lieutenant Philips here to talk you through pressing charges, but before that, I need to take a look at that hand. "

CHAPTER 13

Maria pours Theo a cup of coffee as he stumbles into the kitchen. He hugs her and mumbles something incoherently before sitting down at the table.

" Thanks for letting me stay the last couple of nights sis.. I really couldn't have coped with being on my own. I can't believe I've fucked up *so* badly. "

" To be fair, I think most people would have drawn the same conclusion hun. You weren't to know that it was his sister and child. He had not made any effort to tell you what was really going on. I just feel bad for them all. Imagine how scary that must have been? Fleeing your abusive husband and believing you have a safe haven with your brother only to find out that he still managed to track you down. " She says shivering at the thought as she finishes her shot of espresso. " Okay, so I need to get myself motivated, are you okay for me to use the bathroom? I have to be at Waterloo by nine so that I can catch the Exeter St David's train going to Crewkerne station. I need to be at the Tithe Barn by twelve to start getting set up. " She sits down next to him. " Are you sure I can't convince you to come? It will be fun. " She waits for him to answer, willing him with her words. " Come on sweet. "

Theo starts to answer, before stopping mid sentence.

" You know what Maria, fuck it! I'm going to come after all. I mean, putting distance between he and I will be just what I need. Also, let's face it. It can't be anymore difficult than being here in London right now where I could bump into him at any given moment. Plus I haven't seen my dad for months. I'll see him whilst you're at the venue getting ready. " He says as he boots up the internet to book a last minute train.

She leans in and cuddles him so tightly. " Amazing! I'm so pleased that you're coming.. truth be told I have selfish reasons for you coming too, I need you with me because I'm feeling more than a little nervous. "

" Why are you nervous? It's not like you're reliving a childhood nightmare tonight like I will be. " He says smiling as he enters his card details online.

" What I mean is, this is the first professional gig I've ever had to do." She pours another espresso from the coffee machine. " There is a big chance I could royally fuck it up. "

" Don't be silly Maria, there's more chance of me turning straight than you getting food wrong.. You're an amazing chef. " He says supportively.

Maria grabs a piece of toast and marmalade, walks into the living room to turn the television off, when she hears the local news mention a familiar name.

" A man in Crawley was found dead in his home in the early hours of Thursday morning. The deceased, Jonathan Corrigan was thought to have choked on some pistachio nuts approximately one week ago. The neighbours had reported a smell coming from his apartment. The pathology reports will take place next Wednesday. "

Maria sits down heavily in her chair. " I know him, or I should say I *knew* him. I mean we weren't close, but he works...God I keep getting this wrong, he *worked* in my office floor. Always seemed like such a nice, chatty, happy guy. "

" Don't think he'll be too talkative now. " Theo says without thinking. " Sorry, that was bad taste.. I should have at least waited a week to start making jokes about the dead. "

" Don't you see Theo? That could be either one of us? "

" No it wouldn't baby! Or at least it wouldn't be me, because I know how to chew my food properly. Plus I'm good at swallowing." He says saucily.

" Theo, I'm actually being serious here. This sort of stuff happens to single people living alone all the time. Chances are, there are thousands of people in London right now switching over the channel *not* thinking about that poor man's life for more than one minute. "

" What is your point Maria? That people are heartless? " Theo says helping himself to a glass of fruit juice from the American style silver fridge freezer.

" Yes, well that's a given, obviously.. But more to the point, he didn't have *anyone*. Life is too short to keep pushing people away. "

" Still not getting it. " Theo coldly watches the news report.

" I'm saying that you need to fight for Kez." She says dramatically, standing in front of the television, blocking his view.

He turns and walks back into the kitchen. "It's too late Maria. He would never give me a second chance, you saw his face, he was so wounded by me and my accusations."

" it wasn't that bad Hun, really. "

" Please! He looked at me like I'd just confessed that I'd fucked a horse! "

" No he didn't.. Well, maybe a pony, but that's beside the point. He was going through a lot that night. The last thing in the world he wanted was a full blown argument. "

Theo walks into the living room and slumps into the reclining arm chair. " The really stupid thing is, I *should* have believed him. I know in my heart he wouldn't do that. This man talks to me, and I'm half expecting a fountain of golden syrup to erupt from his mouth. The things he says would be seriously cheesy if it wasn't backed up with his pure, soulful heart. I'd do anything to bring that man back to me. "

" Thats what you have to say. Say it exactly like that. Hell, even that makes me want to kiss you! " She says finishing her toast and going to the bathroom to clean her teeth. Her phone beeps on the kitchen worktop. Without checking if it's his or her iPhone, he picks up the phone and reads the message. By the time he realises that it's a message from Reuben, he has already read it:

' Tuesday night was amazing! I'm so glad you gave me a second chance sweetheart. When am I going to see you again? '

Theo rushes into the rectangular shaped topaz coloured bathroom as Maria is about to get into the spacious quadrant shower and holds the phone up to her face in close proximity and says. " Start talking. "

One night after the events of the hospital, Maria was alone in her flat after Theo had been called in to fill in at work. She had been preparing dinner when she was unexpectedly interrupted by a well dressed, gift bearing Reuben knocking at the door.
" Reuben? " She said awkwardly. " I was going to call yo- "
" Now come on Maria, we both know that's a pile of shit. " He said smiling. " It's okay though. I let you down, I know. That's why I'm here."
She paused. " Well.. "
" Maria, that was honestly something that has *never*, ever happened to me before. I don't want to blow my

own trumpet, but I'm amazing in bed! " Reuben said giving her the flowers and two bottles of wine, one red, one white.

" You know me well. " She said pointing to the wine. " Flowers, on the other hand, I don't know how I feel about that. "

" Oh, okay. " He said, his voice deflated.

Seeing the look on his face, she elaborates. " Only because I've never received flowers .. ever. So I don't really, ummm understand them I guess?! "

Looking around the flat, he saw that the kitchen showed signs of food preparation. " Sorry, am I interrupting? "

" No, you're fine, it's just me.. I'm just practicing a few new buffet style things for the school reunion. "

He looked blankly at her. " Of, course I haven't told you. " She led him into the kitchen and gestured towards him to open a chilled French Chardonnay from the fridge. " I have a new job! I figured that I wouldn't stand a chance of getting my job back, so I had to find alternative options, I mean a girls got to eat. "

Reuben, feeling bad that she was correct in her deductions, and knowing that her letter of termination was in the post, smiled apologetically. " I had no idea that you were so creative in the kitchen. Everything smells amazing! "

" Well, let's hope so, since you'll be the one eating it and telling me your honest verdict, I might add. " She said stirring and frying with multiple saucepans.

" I thank you Maria. Not just for letting me experience your culinary flair, but also for letting me have another chance with you. " He said approaching her from behind, kissing her softly on the back of her neck. One hand wrapped around her waist, the other, handed her the perfectly chilled wine.

She continued to stir the pans as the gentle warmth she had felt from seeing him at the doorway had now grown with intensity with every firm kiss he lay on her neck.

" You excite me so much Maria, " He whispered in his low voice. The hand that was holding the glass worked it's way down to her skirt. He slipped a finger inside her tenderly.

Reuben, sensing that Maria wanted him to continue, cupped her passionately. His long, thick fingers rubbed her rhythmically back and forth. He brushed her clit, lightly at first to gently tease her and then formed his fingers to create small circular motions as her body contracted and released as he explored her fully. He knew exactly what he was doing. He knew how to make her want him so badly. He had always known that no matter how sexually independent she had been, he would be the strong powerful Latino lover that she had always dreamt about in the small hours of the morning. She let out a wanting moan and bit her lip as Reuben turned her head around and kissed her, still holding her in the powerful position against the cooker. The hand that had held her waist, then glided smoothly over her erect, tender nipples. Her body, weak with longing, reached back and touched him, feeling the huge throbbing erection yet unable to hold it fully in her grip.

" You weren't this big last time, were you!? Have you been using one of those penis pumps?! "

He laughs. " No, no sexual aids needed. That's why I was so surprised the first time that it happened that way. Normally I'm rock hard and at full length before I cum.. I think it was just that I wanted you so much Maria.. I'll do you right this time, my queen. "

" Just keep doing what you're doing.. You're amazing! " She said turning off the oven, breathlessly turning herself around to fully take his tongue in her mouth.

He picks her up and takes her to the living room where he threw her on to the couch and proceeded to strip in front of her. His rippling muscular chest and arms, shone against the candlelight. He dropped his trousers, revealing his appendage in all it's glory. Maria gasped and clapped her hands like an excited school child, watching the beautiful man in front of her, statuesque, powerful, oozing sexuality.

" Are you ready for me Maria? " He said knowing she was.

" So ready. Now come over here. "

" I'm so happy for you! " Theo says excitedly as she goes on to tell him how he made love to her for a total of six hours, non stop.

She opens the shower cubicle and takes a towel from Theo.

" I know! It was everything that I wanted and needed. I now have a man who can sexually satisfy me, as well as being someone who I *genuinely* like. "

Theo slaps his forehead, realising. " Now I know why you weren't up when I finished work at twelve.. The first night I had to put you into bed otherwise you would have been asleep on the sofa for the night. " He nudges her playfully before changing the subject slightly. " So, did he like the taste of.. your party food? "

Forgetting about the food she had cooked, she laughs in recollection. " I don't know about the amuse bouchés but he definitely amused my bush...Seriously Theo, I couldn't even walk the next day! I woke up thinking that I'd had surgery! "

He points at her phone, bringing it to her attention. " So when are you going to see him again? " He says, just as he has an idea. " No, don't answer that. He should come this weekend too! "

" Already thought of that, and I would, but he wasn't a member of your school year silly! "

" That doesn't matter, he will have a masquerade mask on anyway. " He says reasoning with her.

" What do you mean a masquerade mask?! Is this a school reunion, or is it some kinky sex orgy?? "

" No silly! Basically, the invitation states that you have to be wearing a mask with a name badge. When you recognise the names of the people you want to speak to, you ask them to reveal themselves. See? "

" Ah I understand now! So what you're saying is, because no one will recognise him, they won't ask him to take his mask
off. "

" Exactly! " He says getting in the shower as she gets out.

" I'll call him now! I know he's got two day off starting today. Don't be long now T! I know you normally take a month to get ready but we have to be ready to go soon. "

Half an hour later, and the two close the door behind them and wait outside for Reuben to take them to Waterloo station, bound for the south west.

The sun is shining so brightly and the air feels warm enough that it could easily be mistaken for a summers day.

" I think that's him in the distance. " Maria says smiling from ear to ear.

Theo seeing her lustful wide grin, looks straight at her.

" Don't you get any ideas about disappearing to the toilets on the train and fucking him. "

" Thought never crossed my mind. " She says wickedly.

The sleek grey metallic porsche 911 convertible, pulls up next to them and Reuben, dressed head to toe in full Armani suit, steps out to take the luggage from them both.

" You know it *is* allowed for you to be seen in a t shirt and jeans when you're not in work, right? " Maria says, teasing him.

He looks down at his attire and then worriedly back at them.

" Damn it! I'm over dressed, aren't I? "

" Not for tonight, you aren't baby, but you *definitely* are for a three hour sweaty train journey to Exeter. " She says kissing his unsuspecting lips. " Do you own anything more casual? "

" Of course I do." He says, noticeably annoyed at himself. " I'm not completely rigid. " He opens a bag from the boot and pulls out a white T shirt and diamond dark blue Levi's 506 jeans and proceeds to strip off in front of them.

Theo, enjoying the view, smiles to himself as Maria first slaps him, and then shouts at Reuben. " Hun! *In the car!* Change in the car! "

" I did not expect that-, " He says pointing in Reuben's direction. " to be under all that.. Wow! You *are* a lucky girl aren't you? "

" Theo! Please! You're coming across as one of those trench coat perverts who lurk in the bushes! Kindly avert your eyes!! " She says half joking.

Reuben hearing her objections, shyly introduces himself to Theo, extending his hand. " Hey Theo, Maria talks about you all the time. I know we briefly met the other night at the bar, but it's a pleasure to meet you properly. "

" Likewise. " He says trying to shake his hand whilst not staring at Reuben's half naked body.

The three of them, bags successfully loaded into the luxurious sports car, talk excitedly as Reuben confidently negotiates the busy roads of London. Theo seems genuinely surprised and charmed by Reuben's way. The stern, professional exterior that Maria had always described him as on a day to day basis had now, all but melted away.

"We're here! Here's the turning! Take a left ! " Says Maria loudly.

" What gave it away sis? Was it the big sign saying Waterloo station, or was it the sound of the trains arriving and

departing? " Says Theo dryly as Reuben unsuccessfully attempts to disguise his laughter.

" You can't talk, mister ' I can't find my car in the space I've only just parked in. ' " Maria retaliates comically.

Theo laughs it off before saying. " My memory may be not that good, but at least I have a sense of direction. "

" What's that supposed to mean, dear brother? "

" Well, let's just say I'm not the one that thinks Stonehenge is just a few minutes down the road from Cardiff! "

" Shut up you shit! You know I was never good at geography! " She says play fighting with him as the car comes to a halt. Reuben removes the luggage from the boot, his previous amusement, now erupting into belly laughs.

" You two are both hilarious around each other. I bet there's never a dull moment when you are both in the same room? "

" It's true..I can't deny it.. we are amazing. " Theo says smiling at Maria as they collect their tickets and board the train at an impossibly busy Waterloo station. " I have a feeling this weekend is going to be just as amazing too. "

Two and a half hours later, their lungs cleansed from the sticky air of the Big Smoke, they arrive in sunny Somerset. The serenity of Crewkerne railway station, visually confirming that they truly are indeed, miles away from their fast paced way of life. The expansive canopy above sheltering the one remaining platform, shields them from the mid day glare from the sun. They make their way through the red doors, into the ticket booking and waiting area, out onto the other side.

" So, what time is your dad meeting you Theo? " Maria says orientating herself, looking back at the grade two listed building.

" Should be any moment now. Do you realise I haven't seen him for about four months? "

" I'm sure it will be lovely though. " She says preoccupied with the list of taxi firm numbers that Veronica had emailed over to her. They walk up the slight slope towards the main road away from the station to get some better reception. She stops suddenly and starts to dial before kissing Theo goodbye on the cheek. " Don't be too late Theo! I need you to be there for support. "

"He hugs her back. " Don't worry, if my dad is anything like he normally is, he will be trying to get rid of me so that he can get back to fucking his partner. "

" Like father, like son.." She says knowingly with a smile. " Give my love to him! " Within minutes, Maria books the taxi and before long a car approaches with the familiar Radio Cabs placard sitting atop the roof. " *Oh! And call Kez.. I know you want to!!* "

Theo leans up against the red telephone box to the right of the entrance to the station. The sound of the moderate traffic coming and going on the main road mixed with that of the departing train further pushes his thoughts of Kez to the forefront. He thinks of how representative it was of the last couple of days in London, one minute it's there, the next, it's gone. He has no choice but to acknowledge the whirlwind romance and how refreshingly quick it had come to him, until those last moment when his history with Andrew damaged his perceptions of Kez.

" Theo! " The unmistakeable sound of his dad's warm energetic voice breaks his musing.

" Dad! How the hell are you?! " He warmly hugs the tall, Mediterranean looking man. " I missed you! "

" You're looking good as ever. Told you we have strong genes, didn't I? " He says jovially referring to his older, equally handsome self. " I bet you have a string of men after you as usual? " He pretends to look over his shoulder, waiting for such a man to arrive.

" Very funny dad.. Well, I was seeing someone, before I fucked it up.. How about you? Last time I was here...What was her name.. Was it Aurora? " He quizzes.

" Oh shit! It really has been *ages* hasn't it? Nope the new one is in the car right now. She's just dropping me off so we can both have a drink. "

Theo laughs heartily. " The new one?! Dad she's not a replacement gasket for a car! She's a woman."

" Believe me son, I'm fully aware that she is *all* woman. " He says nudging him hard. " Anyway, her name is Sapphire. "

"*Sapphire??* Now you're just making it up, aren't you? Who calls their child that. That has to be bordering on child abuse! "

" Don't be mean Theo, all three of the sisters have names of precious stones. "

Theo shakes his head, happy for the comic relief his dad always created. " Doesn't make it alright though. I mean, what must it have been like when they were kids? Actually, I can see it now, ' Diamond, dinners ready! ' Or ' Remember, be back here no later that ten tonight Rose Crystal. ' "

" I know what you mean, it doesn't roll off the tongue so easily when it comes to dirty talk in the bedroom. " He says leaning in to whisper in an exaggerated theatrical way. " She is really great though, she's a lot of fun. "

Theo, looking at him, his head tilting to the side says. " *Dad...*"

" Oh stop being such a spoil sport. " He says looking over at her as he waves, giving her the confirmation that she can leave.

" There's no reason to think that she isn't perfect for me. It's only been a few months. "

Theo watches as she turns the car around and drives off into the distance, tooting the car once. " You know she's it's not going to last, because if you felt that it would, then you would have introduced me to her. "

" Damn ! Why do you gays have to be so damn perceptive! It's like I'm in a psychiatrists chair when

I'm around you, son. " He says warmly hugging Theo again whilst brushing the top of his head. " Don't make it so long next time, alright? "

He nods in agreement." Okay, now let's get a drink. I *really need* one right about now. "

" Why is that then? " He says walking with Theo to the unmistakably bright white pub in the middle of a stream of dull grey and beige houses situated at the bottom of the road. Theo looks up at the hanging sign, and the exterior entrance wall confirming the name of the pub, ' Old Stagecoach Inn '. The title, written in a Proclamate style font, appears to be as old and quaint as the pub itself. They are greeted warmly by the bar staff as they walk through the black door into the establishment.

" Things not going so good ? What's happening with you? The last I knew, you were with that guy Andrew. " He says flippantly as he orders a Brugs Wit for himself before turning to Theo to ask him what he would like. " That was his name, wasn't it? "

" Yeah he turned out to be a prize cunt. " He says pointing to an rich Merlot.

" Ouch! Those are some harsh words.. What did he do? " He says taking a sip of the fruity citrus beer.

" Betrayed me, cheated... *And* might I add , with a woman."

" I *never* did tell you, but he did give off a really bad impression of himself. "

" Dad! You only met him once!! "

" I know I did! But, when he used to talk about girls, he seemed *too* into it. "

Theo looks blankly. " Sorry? You've lost me. "

" No disrespect son, but you wouldn't see it.. You don't hunger for pussy.. It's like the difference between a meat eater and a vegetarian. " He takes another sip. " Deep down you *always* know where your heart really lies.. "

" So why the hell did you not tell me? You could have saved me a lot of heartache. " He says smiling at his dad's complete honesty.

" Theo.. Have I ever dictated to you anything in your life? "

" No, but it would have been nice if I'd known your theory about him. "

His dad walks him over to the table in the corner, pint in one hand, Theo's arm in the other. " You just have to find the one. "

" Okay, but what, in your opinion, is ' the one ' "

" The one is the one. " He leans back in his chair, strokes his beard, taking a few moments. " Once you decide to let someone truly see you, that's when it becomes real. Something tangible. " His eyes glazing up with moisture. " The one is someone who knows your thoughts even before you do.. The one is someone who knows all your insecurities and turns them into something positive, something beautiful , rather than using them against you when you are at your lowest point. Someone who gets you completely, on every level." He wipes his eyes with a napkin. " Someone who, when you wake up in the morning, you look over at them and the love you feel overwhelms you so much because you see your entire life with them.. " He looks at Theo for a good ten seconds before taking the strength to open his mouth without crying. " Someone like your mum. "

Theo, seeing his dad start to well up, clasps his hand over his so tightly. " I miss her too dad, there's not one moment that passes by that I don't wish I could see her again. I miss her *every* day. "

" I know son." He dries his eyes. " Some people are lucky enough to get their ' forever ' more than once in their lifetime.." He looks out of the lattice design window up to the sky. " For me, I'm just glad I was blessed to have been able to tread the same path as her for those blissful forty two years. " He smiles, looking back at him, his eyes glistening. You know what though, we didn't just have each other. We were lucky to have been given the most beautiful gift anyone could have ever wished for, that gift was you Theo. "

" Please dad, are you trying to kill me right now? " He says fighting the tears.

" She would have been so proud to see you today. To see you as the respectful, loving kind man that you have grown into. " He sniffs resolutely. " and everything I've talked about ... that's what I want for you...Promise me something son. Don't ever settle for anything else, just find *your* happiness, *your* strength, the man that makes *you* feel so happy to be alive. "

Theo, taming his cracking voice with a swig of wine, speaks. " That's just it dad, I already have.. I just need to make it right, I don't know how.. but I need to find a way to get him back. "

He looks him in the eye. " I find it very hard to believe you would ever do anything intentionally to hurt anyone you care about. Have you really done anything wrong? Or is this all based on misunderstandings? "

" Without a doubt, it's all my fault... I was stupid. "

" Why? Enlighten me. "

" I foolishly let myself believe this wonderful man would ever hurt me.. Dad, he truly made me feel like I was everything to him... You know I fucking hate Andrew for what he's done to my brain! Bastard!! " He says thumping the table whilst taking another swig. A few locals turn around to look in the direction of the commotion. " I hate that man so much. "

His dad, un clasping Theo's fist with his hand, looks him squarely in the eyes." As your friend, *not* just your dad, I'm telling you, *you need to call him.* "

Theo looks at his phone, then at his dad, and then instinctually starts to dial.

CHAPTER 14

" Theo! You need to get here now! My fucking cocktail bartender has bailed on me! Apparently, he strained himself making a Blue Lagoon whilst trying to impress some stupid girl so she would sleep with his even stupider ass! You have to help me! Please tell me You'll be here soon?! Okay, call me back when you get this.. Love you. "

Maria puts the phone back down on the bar counter. She pours herself a shot of neat vodka to steady her nerves and walks out into the magnificent main hall of the Tithe Barn, surrounded by the grounds of Haslebury Mill. The beautifully crafted walls made from Ham stone, matched with the majestic oak doors and the blue Lias floor, create the perfect gothic setting for the approaching masquerade ball.

The four medieval chandeliers, suspended from what must be a thirty foot high ceiling, commands her attention with their size alone. She takes a moment to view the stage at the front of the building. Although fitting in with the ambience of the barn's olde world design, it houses an out of place, yet impressive sound system with an expensive DJ booth off to the right. Maria smiles optimistically at the almost regal feel of the venue of her first catering gig, but is soon brought back to reality by a less than subtle Reuben entering the barn.

" Relax Maria, this is only one small thing... there are a lot of hours in between now and the reunion in which things could go wrong. " He says smiling.

Maria shoots him a sharp look, before contemplating taking a shot of each liqueur from the bottles fixed against the slab of golden oak wood that stretches across the back wall of the bar.

" Okay, I guess that it's too early to joke about that. " He walks over to her and gives her a tentative hug. " He will be here, as will I, so *if* anything goes wrong, *we* will be here to correct it schnookums. "

Maria looks directly at him, laughing awkwardly. " Umm, schnookums? I'm sorry, I wasn't aware that I've suddenly turned into a *new born baby* in the last few minutes?!? "

Rueben, lowering his head like a child chastised, rephrases. *Love*, I meant love... Or is that not acceptable in the dictionary according to you? "

Maria unclenches and smiles back at him. " I'm sorry, I just want it to be perfect... It's really important to me. This is my first big catering job, plus I don't want to fail like... well... *you know*. "

" You'll be fine.. Just try to not sleep with anyone... Except me." He says lightheartedly.

" Asshole! " She says slapping him on his chest playfully before returning to his warm embrace. " You're good for me, you do know that Reuben? "

" I know Maria, I'm like cod liver oil and B vitamin complex tablets. " He says nodding , his eyes smiling.

" Listen! Im trying to be serious here. " She looks up at his beautiful hazel eyes. " You help me stay feeling level when I'm all kinds of lopsided."

" I'm sure there is surgery we can look into to fix that. " He quips. Sensing that she is starting to pull away from him, he kisses her on her forehead before looking down at her. " Hey, I'm kidding... I'm just being the boyfriend you should have had years ago. "

She looks at him in awe. The positivity and love he expresses with every word, makes her forget where she is for a minute before the bubble bursts when a dishevelled looking man with a clipboard enters the bar.

" Delivery for Ms Martinez. " He says monotonously, making his way over to her and handing her the delivery note. " Sign here, and here please. "

In front of her, on a sac truck piled four feet high with a second delivery of groceries and meats, lay a gift card, a case of expensive champagnes and an assortment of chocolates from Hotel Chocolat.

"Something you're not telling me Maria? Do I have competition? " Reuben says smiling.

" Of course baby, didn't you know the best way to woo a woman is by giving her thick slabs of steak and countless chicken breasts? " She says, teasing him as she picks up the card and reads :

Darling! Just a little good luck wish for your first catering job. The first of many.

Good chi and well being.
Veronica

P.s Could you do me the biggest of honours and cater for my daughters wedding. I already know the food will be exquisite.. Don't worry, you don't have to answer right now, it's a long way off,about a year to be exact.

" How sweet of her! " She says handing Reuben the note as she takes the packages to the kitchen and tips the delivery man. " You could take a few tips from her.. That's how a boss should be. " She says teasing him. " Oh! And I have another job lined up too! Things really couldn't be any better. "
" Well, I don't know why you'd want me to be sending random   flowers and sweet treats to your former colleagues. If that's what will make you happy though, I'll send some, begrudgingly, to every woman on my office floor."
" I'll pretend I didn't hear that. " She says unpacking the meats and putting them in the fridge storage room. She looks at her watch. " Reuben, do you think you could start calling some agencies to see if they have any spare staff free for tonight? I'm just worried in case Theo can't do it for whatever reas- "
Her sentence, cuts short when a familiar voices chirps in.

" Okay, three questions: Where are the lemons and limes being kept? How well stocked are we for alcohol, and what the hell would you have done if I hadn't been here? " He says excitedly as he swiftly enters the venue.

Maria, seeing Theo at the opposite end of the room, runs over, nearly knocking him over as she cuddles him.

" Please tell me you got my message and that was your cute way of letting me know you're saving my ass? "

" Of course it is sis. Either that or it's because I'm so stressed out about tonight that I wanted to know where everything was so I can get tanked as quickly as possible! " He says sarcastically, taking a handful of nuts from the counter.

" Thank you, thank you, THANK YOU *a million times T*. I owe you big time! " She says releasing him, but then grabbing his hand and leading him behind the bar.

" Nah, you don't owe me.. *I owe you..* " He says winking.

Maria, realising instantly he was referring to her instruction to call Kez, yelps excitedly. " *You called him!* That's *so* great. What did he say!? "

" Well, we talked for ages, he apologised, and then I apologised, then he apologised again unnecessarily, so I did the same back. " He says gesturing wildly with his hands. " Only weird thing, was when he suddenly said he had to go abruptly.. But don't worry, I'm not going to let myself get into some crazy paranoid ' Alfred Hitchcock movie ' state of mind. "

She points at him smugly. " *See*, you two are meant for each other. You're both so disgustingly sweet and polite that no one else would be able to stand either one of you without the aid of industrial strength ear plugs. Either that or a huge shot of insulin. " She says processing the rustic olive and walnut bread to go in the stuffed mushroom filling for the magnificent feast to come.

" I never thought I'd hear myself saying this, but now that I'm here, I can't wait. I have to admit though I *really* can't see how they're going to make it look any more fantastic that it already does. Do you know when they are coming to pimp it up? "

" Well, what with the barman cancelling on me, and then the food incident, it really hasn't been at the forefront of my mind. "

" Food incident? What? Has something else gone wrong already? " Theo says checking that the huge ice buckets under the bar are filled.

" Basically, I took the smallest bite of a smoked salmon and Creme fraiché Bellini that I was testing out, and a few moments later I was desperately trying to make it to the toilets before I redecorated the walls with my own designs. " She says rolling some California rolls and fresh tuna nigiri before placing them alongside the ever increasing selection of home made sushi. " Naturally, my first thought was, have I just given myself food poisoning? So I made Reuben have a mouthful of the same thing, and he appears to be fine. "

" That doesn't always mean anything though, I've always had a cast iron stomach when it comes to food. " He says, casually helping himself to a chorizo empanada. " What would give *me* mild indigestion could *kill* another person. "

Maria, looking panicked and worried, invites Theo to try a Bellini to put her mind at ease.

Theo takes a tentative mouthful and chews. His eyes roll with pleasure and his mouth salivates at the perfect combination of smoked fish and black pepper, the lemon juice cutting through with it's acidity.

" Oh my god! These are out of this world! In fact, I'm pretty sure I just came. " He says checking his groin before taking another one off the plate and devouring. Maria takes a minute to watch him, making sure there are no adverse reactions, before speaking. " So I think it must have just been nervous stress that caused me to react that way. I can't see anything else it could be. "

Theo nods in agreement before looking at his watch. " Okay, there's a lot of preparation to do before tonight, so let's get to it." He looks at the selection of white and rosé wines and bottled beers displayed in the fridge. He is surprised by the wide array of liqueurs

and spirits at his disposal on the aforementioned wall.
" This is impressive. Anyone fancy a Cosmo Russe? "

Maria and Reuben answer simultaneously in agreement as Theo takes a shot of Grand Marnier and Raspberry Vodka and then offsets it with the sugar syrup, lime juice and a hint of cranberry juice. He mixes their cocktails before handing it to them, ice cold.

" Can I help at all Maria? " Reuben says sipping the perfectly balanced cocktail. " I feel useless sat here, drinking away. "

" It's so kind of you love, but this is something I have to do on my own. After all, I won't be able to have you with me at every catering job I do. "

" Oh, I don't know, I think I'd look rather fetching in an apron and chefs hat, don't you? "

" You would look great in anything. " She says proudly as she flours and breadcrumbs chicken strips on mass.

" *Or nothing..* " Theo whispers merrily, nudging Maria who nudges him right back.

Rueben, slightly embarrassed at feeling like the pieces of meat Maria is handling, swiftly makes his excuses. " Okay, okay, I know when I'm not wanted." Reuben kisses her lightly on her lips and wanders off into the barn as the two best friends prepare for the night.

As the hours go by, Maria chops and slices, cooks and stirs whilst Theo, adapts the bar to his personal style, making sure every beverage is clearly at his disposal. The two work away, oblivious to the fact that the organisers of the event have been and gone. The barn, now redecorated, remains unnoticed by the two of them. After meticulous attention to detail, the magnificent selection of food is ready to be served and it is only then, that the two take a well deserved break.

" I want you to know, I really like Reuben, " Theo says as Maria opens her mouth to interject. " and before you say it, it has *nothing* to do with that ridiculously incredible body of his. " Seeing that he had predicted what she was going to say, he continues. " I think he is really good for you, he seems to really understand you. "

" Glad I have your blessing *dad*. " She says cheekily.

" Oh and hallelujah that you've found one that can actually satisfy you, this time around. "

" Very true! " She says putting her watch right under Theo's nose. " Look Theo, you had better get changed and get ready for tonight, the guests will be arriving in about half an hour. It's almost eight o clock! Chop, chop! "

Maria walks into the room, and it's only then that she sees the full extent of the decorators handiwork. She glides across the floor to the left hand wall and lays the platters on the beautifully decorated, decadent tables. Each one covered with a satin gold tablecloth with a vintage French candelabra set near the back of the wall, further illuminating the sumptuous food.

Reuben, directly opposite to the stage at the other end of the room, takes a phone call whilst pacing back and forth on the mezzanine, in an authoritative manner. She stares at him, smiling proudly. The feeling of contentment washes over her. *Finally! A man that even my dad can get on board with.*

He waves at her and smiles broadly as he finishes his call and joins her. " Right, that's all my business calls for today... Time for a drink. It's going to be a good night. "

A thirty minute clothes change later and Theo, dressed in a white fitted silk shirt, black waistcoat and shimmering gold tie, looks out into the now crowded room from the side door of the bar, hidden from view. He is amazed by the opulent gold and silver coloured drapes alternating tastefully against every wall, shimmering incessantly. Small strips of deep purple ribbon intertwine with the wooden railings of the stage, conveying a feeling of grandeur.

Theo takes a deep breath. Seeing the decorations, he can't help but be transported back to memories of the equally beautiful surroundings of his own school prom moments before it was to about to begin. He had convinced himself that he would attend the dance, months before the actual date had arrived. He had chosen his outfit and booked his appointment at the barbers. He had even rehearsed what he would say to the bigoted kids who had bombarded him on a day to day basis with homophobic slurs.

In fact, he had spent months preparing himself for what should have been a wonderfully joyous occasion only to turn and walk away from all the festivities before they had even started. Within minutes of walking into the ballroom, he was faced by the sea of whispering, gossiping teenagers all being led by the one and only Kieran. He remembers the feeling of being too tired and too weak to take one more minute of their abuse. If only he could have been the man he was today, back then. He would have shown them all that there was nothing for him to have needed to apologise for. No reason for him to excuse his existence. Feeling the tears burning angrily in his eyes, he pulls the masquerade mask down over his face and walks out into the ball room to offer the complimentary Prosecco.

As Theo walks tall through the crowds of people, he starts to notice the reactions from his class mates as they double take upon seeing his name badge. At first, they would smile happily when presented with a glass of free alcohol, but the toothy smiles would soon turn to apologetic, regretful closed mouths. Each one struggling to find the words to say sorry. As each person attempts to talk, or make excuses for their behaviour in the past, Theo maintains his straight face. He smoulders inside as he relishes the feeling of finally making *them* feel like second rate citizens. No longer did they have control over him. In fact, after a quarter of an hour of serving the expensive bubbly, he was actively *trying* to find Kieran. Kieran, the once powerful ring leader, Kieran the extreme bully intent on preventing him from having one moment of peace. Kieran the tyrant who turned everyone against him so that all they saw was his sexuality.

He continues to scout the huge room until all of the flutes have disappeared from his server, then returns to the kitchen to refill, only this time with canapés.

" Sis! You have done a fantastic job! Everyone can't stop talking about your food. It's a total resounding success! "

" Really? They love it? " She trills waiting for further confirmation from him.

He looks at her dead in the eyes. " More than you love me. "

She starts to smile widely before suddenly reaching her hand to her mouth and then running in the direction of the toilet.

" Okay, okay, I guess that was more than a little cheesy. " He says giggling to himself before realising the noise of retching and being sick, shows him that her actions are genuine.

A few minutes later she reappears, her colour returned, but looking heavy eyed.

" That's the second time today. " He puts his hand to his mouth. " Fuck! Are you pregnant! "

" Don't be silly! " She says unconvincingly. " That's ridiculous! "

" Is it really Maria? It's definitely not food poisoning and one minute you're feeling fine, and then all of a sudden you get waves of sickness..Is it really that out of the question? Can you tell me, with complete confidence that you used protection with Leon and Reuben? "

Maria, grabs her cheeks and temples with her forefingers and thumbs. " Shit! "

" What Hun? " Theo says, searching her face for answers.

" I don't want to sound like a whore, but I *genuinely* had forgotten about Leon.."

" Wow! You *are* a slut. " He says laughing inappropriately without thinking before swiftly correcting himself. " Fuck! I didn't mean that, it was just.. Enough.. So, have you heard anything from Leon? Have you called him? I think he would really appreciate a call. "

" I don't know, should I ? " She says watching the door in case Reuben comes back through. " Two suicide attempts in one year, is more than I'm willing to feel responsible for, if I add *this* on top, it's almost a certainty! "

" Have you told Reuben about him? I'm guessing you haven't since at this point in time, you look like you're hiding from a grizzly bear with the way you're crouched down and whispering. "

" Come on Theo! You can hardly blame me! I mean how would that conversation start... ' so the night that I was suspended from work I slept with my ex who I had a miscarriage with, and this in turn triggered him to attempt to kill himself, and now I may or may not be pregnant with his or your baby! What do you think?! " Maria says, going red in the face.

" Breathe Maria ! " He thinks hard for a minute, " Of course! I still have the pregnancy test in my coat pocket I bought for Connor! "

" *What???* " Maria shouts, forgetting that she was whispering moments before. " Not one part of that sentence made any sense?? "

Theo giggles, realising how strange it must have sounded, explains. " Long story, but Connor, that barman from my work place I told you about, thought he got some girl pregnant and he wanted her to take it then and there. There's two in each box, so you do the math. I'll go get the test, and you can slip off and do it later. Are you okay for a minute? "

" Thanks Hun, " She says taking a seat for a minute. "I really don't know what I'll do though if I am.."

Hours go by and the once refined party atmosphere transforms into club like proportions as the lights drop and the music increases in volume. Theo, walking around the perimeter of the room, continues to collect empty glasses and take drink orders. A few brave people attempt to engage Theo in trivial conversation, but are met with his strong silence and an intentionally near full face harlequin black and white mask. One of the guys, Jamie Saunders, stands up, meeting his gaze through the mask.

" Come on Theo! It was years ago, we were all stupid kids! It's not like we were doing it off our own backs. If there's anyone you should be mad with it's Kieran! He's the one that had the real disdain for you. " He says swaying drunkenly.

Lifting off his mask sharply, Theo's stern, unflinching face meets him nose to nose. " *Don't you think I know that! It's just typical that he is too chicken shit to even turn up tonight to give me the satisfaction of that confrontation !!* " He says returning his mask to his face before turning to walk away.

Gemma, Jamie's childhood sweetheart from school follows after him and taps him on the shoulder. " What are you talking about Theo? "

" Are you deaf? I said, *he's* not here. " He says, agitated.

" Yes he is. I have just seen him heading to the men's restroom. He's the one with the tailor made mask covering his face completely. It's got a cracked white porcelain design on it, with ornate feather effect swirls around the chin and eye area. " She says calmly.

Without turning to acknowledge her, Theo swiftly makes his way to the other side of the room to the toilets. His heart full of fire, the determination thankfully not visible to the rest of the room. Maria, seeing him striding with purpose, rushes over to him.

" Whats wrong? " She says.

Without words, Theo gives her the confirmation of the answer to her question she already knew.

" I'll take care of it. " She says quickly as she grabs the ' do not enter' sign and puts it squarely in the middle of the doorway.

He takes a controlled, deep breath before walking into the men's toilets. He quickly notices that there is nobody occupying the cubicles, just a man washing his hands with the described mask. Theo resolutely stands right next to the tall muscular man and reads the name tag Kieran Jaimeson, in the mirror. Without thinking, adrenalin surging and coursing through his veins, he rips his own mask from his head. His face, portraying the same hatred as before with the man in the ballroom, but this time, with a higher level of intensity.

Kieran jumps back at the sight of Theo, as if electrocuted,   nearly losing his balance. He straightens up only to fall down to his knees on the black and white chequered floor, his hands covering his mask.

Theo, taken a back by the bully's reaction, takes a moment to reassert himself.

" Why are *you* on the floor, you bastard! Don't you *DARE* tell me you actually have a conscious, cos there is *no way* in this world I'm believing that, you fucking asshole!! "

Kieran remains on the floor, shaking. His head firmly locked into his hands.

" Get up off the floor!! " He shouts down at him, spitting unintentionally from the anticipation of this day arriving.

" Take your fucking mask off so I can see what the truly cowardly, waste of space, I have despised for so many years, looks like!! You at least owe me that! "

The man, still silently holding his head, shows no signs of removing his mask. Theo pulls him roughly to his feet by his underarms, and the two fight. Kieran desperately try's to stop Theo's rage from succeeding in removing the mask, until eventually he rips of the expensive head piece.

As if shot, Theo recoils in horror.

There is front of him, the truth so irreversibly and cruelly revealed. Instead of seeing the face of the man he so desperately hated throughout his life, there in front of him, tear stained and upset, was the face of the man he had fallen so utterly in love with.

Kez.

Trancelike, Theo stares at him. Every brick in the wall, every light in the ceiling, every noise from the cisterns and every sensation in his brain slowly starts to decay and crumble away.

Kez speaks, his voice audibly trembling. " Theo, I swear I had *no idea! Y*ou have to believe me..I was so mortified when I saw that you were *him* when you removed your mask! " His lip quivering. " I saw your name badge when I walked by you earlier when you were serving from the drinks tray. I was trying to avoid you all night, because I knew that you would still be angry from the pain I caused you when we kids. Theo, I promise you that I didn't know you were that scared boy, just as much as you didn't know I was Kieran... We were so young back then, we were twelve years old, we look *so* different now! If I.. I don't even ... Words can't even begin to express how sorry I am for what I put you through.. I was so stupid! So immature! " He reaches out his hand to touch Theo's arm. Surprisingly, Theo doesn't move. He doesn't try to shake him off, or flinch or step away. He just stands there, the touch of his skin turning from warm and comforting, to clammy and cold.

" Theo, are you okay?! Your skin... It's like *ice..* "

Still no words utter from his mouth. The vague movement of his mouth trying to formulate words with no sound concerns Kez immensely.

" *Please* say something Theo, you're really starting to scare

 me! " He checks under Theo's nose to see if he's still breathing. " Do you want me to get Maria? Just nod if you do! Theo! " The music playing so loudly in the ballroom, drowns Kez's urgent voice. " I'm going to go get her, just wait.."

Just as Kieran is about to leave him, Theo opens his mouth to speak as one single tear falls from his left eye breaking his catatonic state. " I'm fine."

" I don't think you are Theo, I think I need to get you to Maria. "

Theo speaks, his voice so inexpressive, so emotionless. " I said I'm fine. " He turns away, appearing to drift across the room, ghost like, to the sink, all the while Kieran following behind him.

Kieran overcome with emotion, wraps his arms around Theo from behind, begging. " *Please don't leave me..* It took me years to finally find a man who sees me for me.. Please don't leave because of who I used to be... the insecure, ridiculously underdeveloped, horrible person I was before..." He squeezes Theo harder, hanging on as if it was the last time he would ever hold him. " Back then, I couldn't cope with how much of me I saw in you... I knew I was feeling things for you when you used to walk in the classroom ... You used to take my breath away. " He dries his eyes on his Tom Ford black tuxedo, letting out a half hearted laugh. " Do you know the funniest thing? With every punch, and every kick and every awful thing I used to say to you, in my own fucked up way, I was craving you...You never knew I was falling in love with you, did you? Why would you.." He leans in closer to Theo's ear and begs him. " *Please don't leave...* I just don't think I can bear it.... I *know* I can't bear it...To never see your beautiful face in the morning, to never hold you in my arms and feel you next to me. To never experience your warm heart, or the intense surge of love I get with every time I see you smile, or laugh. Fuck! Even when you cry you're radiant! " He takes Theo's hand and pulls it back onto his chest. " Listen baby, really listen. You know... You know.. we *are* soul mates.. Do you hear me? Theo? "

Theo's once tense body starts to shudder, small movements at first, then developing into strong convulsions. Every intake of air follows the most heartbreaking, tearful, audible release Kez has ever heard.

" I'm fine.. I'm fine..." He repeats. Each time more broken, as his vocal chords swell somewhere between inconsolable sadness and uncontrollable love. " I'm fine.. I'm fine.."

Kez, through floods of tears, struggles to find the words.

" If I could baby... I would do anything... Anything to change the hell I put you through... I *would*.. If I could.. You're my angel Theo.. and I never meant to break you... I *love you Theo Morrison.* "

Theo collapses as Kieran catches him in his arms. He holds on to him, although he says nothing. Kez feels the warmth returning to his his lovers body, and holds him tighter. Theo curls his body into him   the

same way he had after the first time they made love. "
I *whole heartedly, completely, utterly love you.* "

Theo, still crying through blurry unfocused eyes, sees
the love in his eyes and reaches up to kiss him as the
two of them reconcile. Their love for each other
irrefutable. He opens his mouth to speak. " My dad
was right, you know? "

Kez, heavy with emotion, holding on as tightly as
humanly possible, looks down his true love. " Really?
In what way
baby? "

" When I was a kid, he said that you were a good
person and that all you needed was someone to show
you love..." He says touching his face. "Now you have
mine.. and I have
yours. "

The two of them, healing each other with every
minute passing by, talk openly and freely about the
past as the music outside continues to pound.

Hearing his phone vibrate, Theo picks himself up off
the floor, takes his mask and stuffs it into the waste
paper bin. He pats his trouser pockets but cant find
his phone. He looks behind him and sees that it has
fallen onto the floor by the sink, where, moments
before, the two of them had fought.

" I'll get it love. " Says Kieran stepping forward to
retrieve it, whilst still holding his hand. He frowns
and smiles awkwardly. " Its from Maria, but it looks
like half a message."

" Why, what does it say? " Theo says drying the last of his tears on his sleeve.

Kez hands him the phone before answering. " It just says ' I am..... "

Printed in Great Britain
by Amazon.co.uk, Ltd.,
Marston Gate.